I0727901

Broken Chains:

A Paranormal Protector Tale

Book 1 in the Heart of Stone series

DEMELZA CARLTON

This book was created with the assistance of a Fellowship from the Katharine Susannah Prichard Writers Centre and a grant from the Western Australian Department of Local Government, Sport and Cultural Industries.

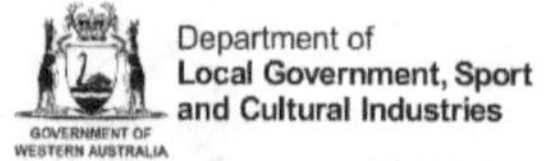

DEDICATION

This one is for Peta – between that retreat in Fremantle, your help with all the research, and egging me on to write it...you totally summoned these boys, too.

ONE

In Catena's perfect world, myths and legends would all be true. Somewhere out there, a fated mate was destined to find her, men in power were capable of making good decisions that benefited more people than just themselves, and her research supervisor would actually tell her what to do for once, instead of magically expecting her to be able to pick the perfect PhD project.

But her world wasn't perfect. Not yet,

anyway.

Professor Bishop spread his hands wide. "The choice is yours, Catena. What sort of research project do you want to spend the next three years studying?"

Catena wished she could sink through the floor before the professor shouted at her for the reply she had to make. "I don't know. What options are there?" It wasn't like she could just pick anything. Archaeology wasn't exactly cheap – she had to pick a project where there was funding, and a dig already planned.

"Well, there are a lot here in Western Australia at the moment – it's a good year for government funding. Fremantle Prison has two projects on the cards for the near future – the hospital and the commissariat. You could start your project before summer does. Or there's the East Perth Cemetery excavation for the new development. Or you could…"

He continued, but Catena's mind drifted. None of them really appealed to her. Worse, whatever she picked, she'd be branded an expert in that for the rest of her life…so it wouldn't just be three years of boredom on a project she had no interest in, it'd be a lifetime of dullness, digging things up she didn't care about. Not to mention she'd become an archaeologist because she'd grown up hearing all the stories about Maria's adventures around the world – Catena wanted to have her own adventures. Stories she could tell Maria about.

Professor Bishop had evidently noticed her distraction. "What about aboriginal heritage? There are a number of rock art projects…"

Catena shook her head. Her family had migrated to Australia – it didn't feel right to be digging up indigenous heritage dating back fifty thousand years or more, when her family hadn't been in the country for more than a few generations.

"Maritime archaeology? There's a team starting to map indigenous settlements on the sea floor from before the sea level rise up in the Pilbara. Big budget for that one, with resource industry funding."

"I don't have my dive ticket," Catena said. Before the professor could remind her that she could have her scuba diving certificate in a matter of days, she added, "And I'm scared of sharks."

Professor Bishop frowned. "So you probably won't be interested in the new Abrolhos study, then. Cataloguing shipwrecks…oh, wait. There's a land one in here, looking at the Batavia sites on one of the islands. No sharks there, unless you go in the water."

Wasn't that the island where a bunch of shipwreck survivors went mad and killed each other over food and water? She'd heard the place was as cursed as Tutankhamen's tomb. Then again, it wasn't like Catena believed in curses or the supernatural, so… "Maybe."

"Ah, it looks like that one doesn't have funding yet – still waiting on budget approval. Still, it's worth considering, so I'll leave it on the list. I'll send it through to your email, so you can have a better look before you decide.

You've only got a month until the proposal deadline, and you don't want to miss it, or you won't be able to get a scholarship. Not everyone gets one, you know. Competition is fierce, and the selection panel only approves the projects they think tick all the boxes best. And even if you do get a scholarship – only a quarter of PhD students actually finish their project on time and graduate. So it's important that you pick the right project – the right project for the selection board, and the right project for you, so you'll finish it."

Catena nodded, even as her tummy clenched into a terrified little ball. She had less than four weeks to make the most important decision of her life…and write a proposal that would convince the scholarships board to pay for it.

Or she could stay an assistant librarian for the rest of her life. Which wasn't bad, but it was hardly an adventure. "I will have my proposal ready on time, Professor. I promise." And she would, because the last thing she wanted was for him to shout at her for not doing it. Or for anything, really – Professor Bishop's volatile temper rarely remained calm for more than ten minutes at a time. In fact, it was a miracle she'd managed to get through this meeting without him getting angry at something. Better not push her luck. She rose to leave.

"See that you – " he broke off as his phone emitted a sound like a police siren. He glared at it, then snatched it up and shouted, "You're not supposed to contact me. My lawyer gave you strict instructions…"

Catena fled, out of the office and down the hall, but even outside she could still hear the professor shouting at his soon to be ex-wife about the disposal of their joint property investments. Half the campus probably knew about Professor Bishop's pending divorce by now, and if they were anything like Catena, they also hoped the matter was sorted and settled as quickly as possible.

She only wished choosing a PhD project

could be as simple.

TWO

Tor opened his eyes to darkness. Then he heard it again, the familiar scrape of stone on stone before it was lifted. Exultation flooded through him – finally, it was time! He would rise and answer the call!

A scratchy voice echoed from deep in his memories: "When I have need of you, I will call, and you shall come. You will protect her, and everything else I hold dear, for that is your purpose. Do you understand? When I call, you will answer!"

But the call did not come.

Instead, a deep, bone-jarring vibration rumbled through earth and stone and Tor, rattling his very teeth in his head.

He was not aware of its ending. Only that he could hear familiar sounds – the rhythmic beat of steel on stone, the clatter of cart wheels, the shouts of men, the crunch of stone surrendering to the superior force of a man, before the very ground started shaking once more.

It must be the middle of the workday, with so much activity about. No wonder the call hadn't yet come, for he could not answer as long as the sun was in the sky.

At night, he would hear the call. And he would answer, as he must. For why else had he been awakened, if not to rise and serve his purpose?

Soon. The sun would sink beneath the horizon, and Tor would rise.

In the meantime, Tor closed his eyes.

THREE

"If you could just shelve those last few returns, you're good to go," Lillian said, gesturing toward the bin under the returns chute. The brimming bin.

Catena sighed. She'd already emptied it twice, but today seemed to be the day every student had decided to return an entire semester's worth of loans, all in one hit. Exams must have started. Then again, shelving books was easier than dealing with panicked students at the help desk, who all wanted to shout at you if you couldn't magically produce the book they needed for today's exam. Never mind that they'd had all semester to borrow it, and now it was out on loan, they expected you to work miracles. "Sure."

Scanning the books into the system so the catalogue would know they were returned took only a few minutes, but returning them took much longer, so that by the time Catena left the library and headed for home, it was already late afternoon, and the sun was sinking fast. Winter definitely wasn't her favourite time of year.

Luckily, she lived close enough to walk home from work, and, luckier still, her street was still closed to car traffic because they were digging up the road to replace the water pipes. So where yesterday there had been a road, now there was a fenced-off dark ditch that stretched all the way down the street, stopping in front of her house. The excavator responsible for the chasm sat proudly beside it, within its fenced off enclosure, as though if it were uncaged it would eagerly begin digging again, extending the trench to the next intersection.

Catena hoped no one would release the beast until she was awake, or, better yet, at work on Monday.

Through the door, up the stairs to the landing above the ground floor shops, one more door to unlock and she was home.

Catena let her bag thud to the floor, too tired to carry it further than the entry. She could pick it up later. Fighting off panic at choosing her future research project AND working fried her brain worse than doing multiple concurrent joint projects during her undergrad degree.

Or maybe it was just manhandling so many books around the library today.

She should be making dinner, but what she wanted was a hot chocolate.

Opening the fridge, she reached for the milk

that wasn't there. Shit. She knew she was supposed to pick something up on her way home, but, like so much lately, she'd forgotten.

She glanced at the darkened windows. Surely she could wait until morning…

But she'd need milk for breakfast, because she didn't do dry cereal. Or she could have toast…

Nope. No bread, either. Better add that to the list. Now she had to go to the supermarket. Luckily, it was still open.

Judging by the slow moving denizens in Coles, not unlike some of the mythical monsters she read about when she had time, she wasn't the only one who'd had an exhausting week. But she had every intention of escaping these zombies and having her hot chocolate sooner rather than later. And with chocolate biscuits, she decided, snagging a pack of Tim Tams from the specials rack at the end of the aisle.

Seeing as she was here, she should probably buy something suitable for dinner. Something she could just whack in the oven to cook while she collapsed on the couch. Even better if there'd be leftovers for tomorrow…

Catena lugged her shopping basket to the cash register, and was soon swinging her fully laden shopping bags as she headed home.

Why weren't the street lights lit yet? She could barely see her feet in front of her, let alone where the footpath ended and the road began. Not to mention what lurked in the shadows between the shopfronts…

She quickened her steps, offering a prayer to whatever deity would listen that she'd make it home safely. Which was probably about as helpful as hoping some mythical monster would save her, should she get into trouble. Or a good-looking monster hunter. She smothered a laugh. Maybe when she got home she should watch –

She stumbled over something in the dark, pitching forward, but she managed to regain her balance instead of faceplanting on the footpath. Hoping no one had seen her tripping over her own feet, Catena kept going.

A shout erupted behind her. "Hey! What do you think you're doing? You broke my guitar case, and…did you just take my money?"

She glanced over her shoulder, just long enough to see someone rise from where they'd been sitting on the ground, before she tucked her head down and bolted for home.

"Oi! You! Stop! You'd better pay for that…"

A woman alone, stopping at the order of an angry man in the dark? Catena wasn't stupid. Instead, she ran faster. This time, when she prayed to whatever deity would listen, she had only one wish – for help.

Just a little bit further, and she'd be safely home. Six more shops. Five. Four. Three…

She looked up, her eyes straining to see the door in the dark. She almost didn't see the huge shadow beside it until it was too late.

Easily twice as wide as she was, and so tall his head brushed against the shop sign suspended from the roof above. And when he stretched his arms out, his fingers surely touched the shop window on one side, and the construction site fencing on the other.

No escape. No way past, and no way back.

If she could only get her keys out in time, unlock the door and slam it behind her…

The keys. Where were her keys?

Strong arms wrapped around her, pressing her against a chest as warm and hard as sun-soaked stone. He whirled her around, spinning a tight circle that only seemed to squeeze her harder, smother her, until she could no longer breathe, and blackness took her.

FOUR

When the call came, it was not the sour, scratchy voice that Tor expected. Nor had he expected the call to come from a woman.

"Someone help me. Please."

It was the barest, breathless whisper, but Tor heard it, for he was waiting. He shot through earth and stone, surfacing on a street that he neither knew nor recognised, but he cared nothing for the street. No, all his attention was on her, for the clarion call came from her lips, as she flew toward him, as if her feet bore wings.

Tor grinned. Her pursuer, the reason for her panic, approached. How dare he even consider harming her. Tor rose to his fullest height, his widest stance, the better to protect her. He swelled until he filled all the available space between the fence and the shopfront, so the pursuer could not pass.

What did she want him to do?

Tor listened hard, for her voice was still the softest whisper.

"Please let me get inside," she repeated. Her eyes darted from him to the door and back again.

Tor bowed his head in acquiescence, as she ran straight into his embrace. His arms closed around her, followed by his wings. Never had he held anything more precious than her trembling form, and he would protect her with every part of him.

Her pursuer skidded to a stop, the whites of

his eyes wide with satisfying fear.

"Begone!" Tor growled.

The pursuer nearly dropped his guitar in his haste to turn and run away, back the way he'd come.

A strange choice of weapon, to be sure. What manner of man wielded a guitar when attacking a woman? If he was some sort of musician, surely he would not risk the tool of his trade so. Then again, he was a fool for daring to chase her in the first place, when she had such a powerful protector.

Ah, but perhaps he had not known?

The musician, if that's what he was, was no longer in sight.

Only then did Tor remember her second command — she wanted to be inside the building.

He held tight to her as he threw his body at the wall, passing through it as easily as he'd travelled through stone to the street. He felt her slump in his arms — she must be a gentle lady indeed, to swoon. He'd best find her a bed or at least a couch to lie on until she awoke – ah, though there were shops below, on the upper floors were bedchambers.

Only one had books upon the table beside the bed, and clothes laid on the chair in the corner. This must be her bedchamber, where she slept.

Tor unfurled his wings, so that he might carry her to bed. Her scent seemed to fill the very air between them, winding its sweet, floral fragrance about him as securely as any spell. He didn't want to let her go.

She gave a little sigh, as if she shared the sentiment.

But sentiment was all it could ever be.

"I am your protector. It is my duty to keep you safe," he said as he laid her on the bed. He tugged off her shoes, then covered her with the eiderdown. The cloth had a strange design upon it, pyramid structures on sand, with a starry sky behind them, as lifelike as though they were real. Like a landscape painting some lord might hang on his library wall. Hardly something to decorate a lady's bedchamber.

Then again, few ladies warranted an immortal protector, so she must be an unusual lady.

Triumph welled in Tor's breast – he'd successfully protected her. Maybe not perfectly, but he'd gotten her home safe.

He hoped she would see it so. If she rejected his service, she might command him to go back to sleep, never to wake again. He would have failed.

But he had not failed. He would tell her so, and pray he did not offend her in doing so.

"It's all right, miss. You're safe," he said softly into the darkness.

Rustling from the bed told her she was awake. She stared at him for a long moment, before squeezing her eyes shut.

Her whispered words carried to him: "Please be gone, please be gone, please be gone…"

If that was her command, then he would be obedient to her wishes. Tor faded into the wall, becoming one with the stone.

He watched and waited for further commands, but she was strangely silent.

She stared searchingly around her bedchamber, as if she did not trust Tor to have done as she asked.

"You're safe," he said from the wall. "It's all right, miss, you're safe."

She gave a little nod, as if she heard him and approved, before she settled down on her pillows and drifted off to sleep.

FIVE

Catena woke in darkness, but there was enough light coming through the window to see that she was definitely in her bedroom. Perhaps she'd dreamed it all – the trip to the supermarket full of zombies, being chased home, and the hulking monster lurking outside her front door.

Okay, put like that, she'd definitely dreamed it all up. It sounded like a mashup of several

Supernatural episodes, with extra zombies thrown in for spice. She should probably watch less TV for a while, if her imagination was conjuring up such craziness when she slept.

She must have come upstairs, decided to lie on the bed for just a moment, and fallen asleep. Wouldn't be the first time.

"It's all right, miss. You're safe."

Catena froze. The voice was male, and definitely in the room with her. If there was a man in her bedroom, then no matter what words he said, she was anything but safe.

There! A shadow in the corner, behind the door. Just as huge as the one she'd seen outside, before he grabbed her.

He lunged forward, then stopped, in a sort of half-crouch that she realised was a bow, before he lifted his head to look right at her.

Moonlight darted through the window and wreathed his face, silvering his dark hair.

Yet when his eyes met hers, dark pools in the shadows of his face, something passed between them. It felt like…understanding.

Understanding that she'd imagined a man in her bedroom. She must be going mad.

Catena closed her eyes. When she opened them, she'd see that there was no one else in her room, and he'd be gone.

Please be gone…

Her eyes popped open, and she flicked on the bedside light. See? The corner was empty, with no shadows to be seen.

She turned the light off, then snuggled back down under the quilt. The most sensible thing to do in this situation was to go back to sleep. She evidently needed it, if she was hallucinating strange men in her bedroom.

"You're safe."

See? Even her hallucinations agreed with her. Catena snuggled under the quilt, mumbling his words over and over to herself as she drifted back to sleep.

SIX

"Work hard, and one day you'll earn your freedom."

"Do as you're told, and one day you'll be your own man again."

"Protect her and the property…"

The words swirled in Tor's head, punctuated by the clink of chains, faint memories that were all he knew of his past. Obey, or he'd wear chains again. They'd lock him up forever, and never let him out.

But not if he protected her. Those were his orders, orders he wanted to obey.

And maybe, just maybe, if he could please her, then she would set him free, just like they'd promised. Because while he did not trust the voices in his memory, hers was not one of them.

Instead, she was his future. A future where he swore he would keep her safe.

SEVEN

Between the sunlight streaming through her window – why hadn't she closed the curtains last night? – and whatever it was digging painfully into her thigh, Catena was forced to give up on sleep.

Sunbeams lit up the corner behind the door, chasing away any hope of a shadow, menacing or otherwise. Definitely a dream.

Catena made her way to the bathroom, then

stopped dead at the sight of her reflection. She hadn't slept in her clothes since…whenever the last time she'd come home drunk from some undergrad party, probably back in first year. Shit, she was still wearing her coat, with…yep, her keys, wallet and phone in the pockets. The keys were what had woken her up. She knew she'd been tired, but surely not so tired that she'd forgotten to take her coat off in the house.

Could it have been real?

No. It couldn't have been. Because…if it had, then there'd been a man in her bedroom last night.

She rushed back to her room, checking in the cupboard, under the bed…anywhere that a creature as big as a cat might hide. She breathed a sigh of relief when no man materialised…only to trip over something on the floor where nothing should be.

Her shoes, beside two shopping bags.

It couldn't be.

And yet…

She had to get the milk into the fridge, before it soured. Not to mention all the other things she'd bought…

Seizing the bags, Catena raced downstairs to the kitchen, then busied herself making sure everything went where it belonged. Creating order from chaos, everything in its place, just like in the library. By the time she closed the pantry door on the last pack of Tim Tams, Catena was pretty sure she'd figured out what really happened last night.

She'd gone to the supermarket, been chased by a busker, brought her stuff home, and been so exhausted from running all that way that she'd gone straight up to bed, and zonked out for the night. Then she'd had a bad dream, imagining there was someone in her room, woken up in fright only to find out she was alone, and gone back to sleep.

Yes. It all fitted, all made sense.

That long, dark hair, those eyes that had mesmerised her, those strong arms that had wrapped around her had all been figments of her overactive imagination.

And the remedy?

She wasn't going to watch or read anything out of the ordinary until Monday. No werewolf fated mates romances, no monster hunter TV shows, no superheroes, no science fiction, NOTHING but contemporary romance and documentaries until Monday.

Besides, she had her PhD project proposal to do. There was enough realistic reading to do on that to keep her busy all weekend.

In fact…

Catena grabbed a packet of Tim Tams out of the pantry, wishing she'd bought more. She considered heading back to the supermarket, but the thought of the angry busker out there, who might still be waiting for her, was enough to keep her inside for the foreseeable future.

EIGHT

Catena considered calling her parents and telling them she was sick, to get out of her weekly visit, so she wouldn't have to go outside her house and maybe see the mad busker again.

But she was woefully low on food, and her mother had promised to make cannoli, which Catena couldn't resist, so the clock in her parents' lounge room was just chiming twelve when she stepped inside. It smelled like roast, but Catena had no doubt that it would be accompanied by some Sicilian foods that her father would insist didn't belong on the same table as a traditional roast. It had been an ongoing argument between her parents for as long as she could remember, but as long as he got his roast potatoes and gravy, Dad usually didn't do more than grumble a bit any more.

"Is that you, Cat? Can you come help me serve up?" Mum called.

That was code for Mum needing to tell her something without her father or brother hearing. Catena hoped it wasn't because Dad had had another health scare. If the doctor had ordered him to change his diet so that he couldn't eat something he loved, Dad would be impossible at lunch.

Luckily, for once, Dad's health was fine.

"Your dad's been taking his pills, and his last batch of blood tests were good, so the doctor said he's allowed to eat normally again. Your dad decided he wanted some roast recipe he saw on some TV cooking show."

If there was one thing Mum hated, it was being told how to cook. Catena winced.

Mum only smiled. "I told him I'm too old to be learning to cook new things, especially dipping potatoes in duck fat or some such thing, so if your father wants to eat some recipe he saw on TV, then he must cook it himself."

Catena choked.

"So, your father has made today's roast, and I want you to make sure you say nice things about it. If it's terrible, don't look at me. I have a big pan of eggplant parmesan almost ready, in case you can't eat any of his things."

"And cannoli?" Catena asked.

"Of course! I promised. What with your dad doing most of the work for lunch, I had time to make enough for lunch and a box for you to take home. Enough to last you all week."

Two days, if she was lucky, Catena thought but didn't say. Best her mother didn't know about her bad eating habits. If she knew she'd had a pack of Tim Tams for breakfast yesterday…or that she'd been chased down the street by an angry busker…Mum wouldn't let her leave after lunch. She'd insist Catena move back home, into her old bedroom with its pink-swathed single bed, as if she were still a child and not a grown woman about to start her PhD. Well, if she got the proposal in on time and actually picked a project.

So "Thanks, Mum," was all she said before grabbing a drink from the fridge and heading for the dining room, where she could hear her father and brother in the middle of a heated discussion about something.

The oven timer shrilled, drowning them both out.

"That's for you, Seamus!"

Dad broke off and came toward the kitchen, kissing Catena's cheek on the way. "Good to see you, Cat. You're right on time."

Catena took a seat across from her brother, who was now intent on the screen of his phone. "How's things, Archie? You headed back up to the minesite tomorrow?"

Archie didn't even glance up. "Tuesday, actually. My rotation changeover is on Tuesday. Then two weeks onsite, before I can come home again."

Catena knew it paid well, but she couldn't imagine working such long hours, so far away from everyone and everything. She suspected he liked it as little as she would, but the last time she'd asked him, he'd snapped that it paid better than archaeology, which she had to admit was true. But there was more to life than work and money…

With a lot more of Mum's help than Dad would ever dare admit to, he finally managed to get lunch on the table, and it wasn't anywhere near as bad as it might have been. Dad had followed the recipe to the letter, which had resulted in a slightly singed roast beef that was at least cooked on the inside, and a mountain of surprisingly tasty potatoes.

Catena gave compliments where they were due, did due justice to her mother's eggplant parmesan, and barely managed to find space for some of the cannoli before she was too full to move. She silently thanked her mother's foresight for offering her a box to take home.

She was just carrying the first armload of plates to the dishwasher when it started.

"What do you think about this zero emissions target thing? Sounds like a terrible thing for the economy," Dad said, cracking open another beer.

"Only if you're a dinosaur like those fossils over in Canberra, who think the economy will collapse if it's not running on coal, like we're still in Victorian times or something," Archie snapped.

"Well, they nixed that carbon tax fast enough. If power bills go up, no one will be able to pay for it, and that'll make the economy collapse. Businesses will go broke."

"No, they won't, Dad. Businesses, especially the biggest players like the mining industry, have been planning for this for decades. Hybrid cars, solar farms, wind, batteries…not to mention mining all the right materials needed to make those things. They don't want to be left behind, even if the government is living in last century. Even you're ahead of them, Dad – you've got solar panels on the roof!"

"Yeah, but are solar panels any good? We only got them because a guy at work knew someone who was doing cheap installation. And the wiring only lasts a few years, which isn't covered by the warranty, so we had to get someone up there last week to replace it all. What's the point of getting solar panels if they're just going to break…"

"Dad! It's not the panels, it's your dodgy installer who's to blame! If you'd gone with the company I told you to…"

As the volume increased on the shouting match between them, Catena tucked the box of cannoli under her arm, waved her free hand in farewell, and headed for the door.

NINE

Maria's nursing home was on her way home. They wouldn't mind if she arrived early. Catena checked the time – visiting hours had just begun. Perfect.

Her godmother was lying in her bed, watching a cooking show, when Catena reached her room. Catena wondered if it was the same one her dad had pulled the roast recipe from.

Catena didn't bother knocking. "Hi, Maria. Mum made cannoli, and I thought you might like some." She brandished the box.

Maria glanced up, squinting at Catena's face for a moment. Catena waited, wondering if she'd recognise her today.

"My god-daughter likes cannoli. Did I ever show you a photo of her?" Maria asked, lifting the remote to turn off the TV show.

Catena sighed inwardly, but summoned a smile. "I'm not sure. What's her name?"

Maria pointed at a photo on the wall beside her bed. "That's her. Catena. Her parents wanted her brought up all Catholic like they were, but she's too curious to stick to such a narrow view of the world. She'll be an archaeologist, like me, just you wait and see."

Catena longed to remind Maria that she was already an archaeologist, finished her honours degree and about to take the next step, but it wasn't Maria's fault she didn't remember. Alzheimer's had stolen her memories from her, and reminding Maria of that fact only resulted in the most creative slew of curses Catena had ever heard, spanning at least six languages, some of them legally dead, and bringing complaints from all over the nursing home at the words the residents did understand. Because when you could swear in over a dozen languages, you could offend everybody.

"What makes you say that?" Catena asked instead. Maria might not remember who she was now, but sometimes she had crystal clear recollection of their time together when she was little.

"She listened to all my stories, every dig I've ever been on. Egypt, Pompeii, Rome, Turkey...that time I made it to Russia..." Maria smiled. "And when she's old enough, I'll see she's all set up, too. I've left her everything in my will. The house...all of it. She'll have someone to look out for her, too."

"I...I mean, she will? Who?"

Maria winked. "The gargoyle, that's who! He's more valuable than anything inside the house, for he'll be her defender. He'll make sure nothing bad happens to her."

The statue on the roof. Catena sighed. Here she'd been hoping that maybe Maria had spoken to some of her old colleagues, someone who might offer her more options for her research than Professor Bishop could.

"Now, where's that cannoli?" Maria asked.

Catena sat down beside her and opened the box.

"Did I ever tell you about the time…"

Maria had, for Catena had heard all her stories, but she never tired of them, so she settled down to listen.

TEN

When the nurses shooed her out of Maria's room and back home, the winter sun enticed Catena out onto the roof on Sunday afternoon, with her laptop and a fresh packet of Tim Tams to go with her cup of coffee. By the time the biscuits were gone, she'd run through Professor Bishop's project list twice, and she was still no closer to picking one.

She wished she could have talked it over

with her family, Maria, or even one of her friends, but none of them would understand. Well, Sibyl would, if she weren't working some ice dig up near the Arctic Circle, where the phone and internet access was next to non existent. The last time she'd called, there'd been so much static, Catena had barely understood any of what she was saying.

Of the ones who were still here, only Alethea intended to go on to do her PhD, and she'd already had her project picked for her – that cemetery dig her company had won a project for. They were paying her to do the actual site excavation, so she'd be crazy not to choose that one. But Catena worked in a library, not a heritage consulting company, so getting her employer to make the decision for her wasn't an option.

Truly, she just wanted someone to tell her what to do, make the decision for her. It could be anyone, just as long as she didn't have to be the one to do it. Well, it should be someone who knew her, and something about the projects, and what would suit her…

"What do you think?" she asked the gargoyle that sat on the edge of the roof. He'd been there since the place was built, her godmother had told her, when she still lived in this apartment, before she'd gone into a nursing home. He knew all the building's secrets, and he'd heard hers since she'd been old enough to talk. It wasn't quite the same as telling him she didn't like peas, or that she'd bitten the first boy she kissed so he'd gone off wailing to his mother, but she knew he'd never told anyone her secrets, because her godmother had told her gargoyles were protectors, fiercely loyal to those under their care. Plus, he never left his eyrie, at the top of the building.

On the day she'd helped Maria pack her things for the nursing home, Maria had pointed at the gargoyle and said that his job was to protect Catena now, because the apartment was hers. Catena had put it down to Maria's advancing dementia at the time, but it hadn't stopped her talking to the gargoyle.

One day, she might get a cat, like her neighbour, but she didn't feel responsible enough to be a pet owner. She struggled to keep Maria's plants alive as it was.

The gargoyle just sat there, looking thoughtful, like he was patiently waiting for her to continue.

Well, she should probably give him all the facts. Even just talking about them aloud might help.

"The interstate and overseas ones, I can pretty much cross off the list right away. It's not like I can afford to travel, or live in another city for a while. Even the ones in Western Australia that are too far to drive to, I can't really do. Anything further than Geraldton or Albany, really. I mean, any of the Pilbara projects are a two day drive, and it's not like I own a four wheel drive, which is pretty much what you need out there.

"So, there are three sites on the list I could probably get to. The Abrolhos dig with the

Maritime Museum, the Fremantle Prison projects, or the cemetery in East Perth. Well, assuming the Abrolhos one goes ahead, I should be able to drive up to Geraldton, and the Maritime Museum team will surely have a boat, so I could even sleep on deck, if I have to. The artefacts will come back to the Shipwreck Galleries, which is only up the road from here, so it's not like I'd have to stay in Geraldton, or out on the islands, and I have heard it's beautiful up there…"

She'd also heard the sharks were massive. Six or seven metres long, big enough to eat her in one gulp.

"As long as I stay out of the water, the sharks should leave me alone."

Not that they'd left the shipwreck survivors alone. According to some of the accounts she'd read, a lot of the survivors ended up eaten by sharks, which was why there were so few bodies buried on the islands.

"I've heard the stories, though. No one wants to sleep on the island, because it's haunted. What with all the people who got killed, and the ones who went mad and did the killing, and then the torture and executions after..." Catena swallowed. The Batavia story was probably one of the most gruesome in West Australian history, and it happened a full two centuries before the Swan River Colony was even settled. "I'm not sure how I'd go if we dug up bodies. I mean, if they were murdered or executed or whatever. I'd have to reread all the translations of the trials and everything, to be able to quote them in my thesis."

Yeah, maybe the Abrolhos one was a bad idea.

"Then there's the East Perth Cemetery. Alethea's already working on that one, so I'd know someone. But she'll be doing her PhD on what she finds there, too, and there might not be enough material for two research projects. It really depends what's in the cemetery. Well, bodies, of course, which have been buried a while. I mean, the Abrolhos bodies are all skeletons by now, but East Perth Cemetery was still in use a century ago, or at least I think so, so the bodies might still be…um, decaying. Or not decaying, depending on how they were buried…"

Who was she kidding? She didn't want to dig up bodies, at the Abrolhos or in a cemetery.

She let out a shaky laugh. "Yeah, I know what you're thinking. Four years from now, do I want to be introducing myself as Doctor Catena Kelly, expert in exhuming bodies? Worse, do I want to continue digging up dead people for the rest of my career?"

The gargoyle, of course, kept his counsel.

"Which leaves the prison projects. They're local, just up the hill from here." She turned and pointed. "They have their own museum collection onsite, so any artefacts we find would stay there, so I'd have no problems accessing them. Both projects are fully funded, so they'll definitely go ahead. Plus, there's more chance of finding something of significance, because the same buildings have been there all this time. The location's perfect, really it is, it's just that…every time I've been up there, on a school trip or whatever, I've just…gotten this really bad feeling.

"I mean, it's a prison. Built by convicts who'd have to live inside it, then made into a maximum security prison filled with rapists and serial killers and people who did such bad things they were hanged for their crimes. The gallows is still there, with a rope and a trapdoor and everything. I could barely stand to stay there for the tours. To have to go there every day to work and dig stuff up, in places where those people spent their days…some of them are still alive, and still in prison, but transferred to Casuarina when Fremantle closed. People so bad, they've been in prison for longer than I've been alive!"

She'd heard the place was haunted, too, almost as badly as the Abrolhos. What sort of place was Perth where the cemetery was the least haunted site on her list?

"Anyway, so those are really the only three options, unless something else magically comes up, which is unlikely. So, what do you think?" She waited barely a moment, before putting her hand up and patting the sun-warmed statue. "No, don't tell me now. It's a lot to take in. We should probably both sleep on it, and you can tell me in the morning."

She gave the statue one last pat, wondering at the warmth under her hand, almost as though the statue was a living thing and not just carved stone, silent and watchful until centuries of weather ground it down to sand. If only it could talk, to tell her all the things it had seen from its eyrie up here...

Catena laughed and shook her head, then headed downstairs to the kitchen to start dinner. Maybe the answer would come to her while she was cooking.

ELEVEN

Tor followed her to the roof, which he was surprised to find furnished like one of the sitting rooms inside the house, with sofas and tables and chairs. She curled up in one of the sofas, with her book-like device that magically showed different pictures at her command.

The best vantage point was a stone statue that faced the front of the building which seemed to be watching the street below. Tor slipped inside the creature, staring out the back of its head at her instead.

At first, she ignored him, as was her custom. He was her servant, far beneath her notice, unless she wanted him to do something. But she hadn't given him a single order since the first night she'd called him into her service.

Perhaps she had no further use for him, and meant to send him back to the darkness from whence he came. If such was her wish, then surely he would feel some pull towards it, like the irresistible compulsion that had brought him to defend her, in her moment of need. Yet the only pull he felt now was toward her. He didn't want to return to his deathless sleep, waiting for a call that might never come. He wanted…

"What do you think?"

Wait, was she speaking to him? She seemed to be staring right at him, as though she could see him hiding in the statue.

Before he could collect his scattered wits to be able to answer her, she began to explain.

She was a scholar, he discovered, with extensive knowledge of history and medicine, or at least the human body. She abhorred violence, for when the very thought of it touched her delicate sensibilities, she shuddered as though a hand had been raised to harm her own person and not some long-dead victim in the past. She was gently born, with a soft but well spoken voice he could happily listen to all day. And while she habitually dresses in men's trousers, a fashion Tor had never heard of before, she wasn't the only one – he could see several other women in the street below wearing the same sort of garb, though there were those who wore skirts, too. Perhaps this was the expected attire for a female scholar. He would not know – he'd never met one before.

The more she spoke, the more Tor became certain that he'd never met anyone quite like Miss Catena Kelly. Even her name sounded like the harmonious rhythm of a chisel chiming on stone…

"So what do you think?" she asked again.

For the second time, his tongue tangled up on him again, with his head a confusion of thoughts as to what he should and shouldn't say, and whether she would permit him to address her by name, like he wanted to, or that a learned scholar like her would actually want to hear the thoughts of someone as uneducated as him…

Then her hand landed on the statue's head and he lost all coherent thought altogether. He strained to reach her through the thin layer of stone that held them apart. The statue bathed in afternoon sunlight, which he dared not touch, unless he wanted to be stuck as this statue's twin until sunset. Then how would he answer her?

"No, don't tell me now. Tell me in the morning," she said, as if reading his thoughts. Perhaps she could, for if she could see him, invisible inside the statue, then it was only a mite further to reach the thoughts inside his head. He would have to guard those, too.

One last wistful pat that Tor wished he could feel with all his being, before she headed inside.

Only when she'd left did pride swell within his chest. She'd given him an order! One he had no idea how he would fulfil, for he'd scarcely understood half of what she'd said, but he would do his best. While she slept, for he did not, he would gather his scattered thoughts and try to find the words to convey them to her, in any way that might help.

For if he could help her now, she might have other commands for him, so that he might remain at her side, watching over her, instead of being sent back into the dark.

And he wanted to stay more than anything.

TWELVE

For the second evening in a row, Tor watched Miss Kelly from the walls of her home. He half hoped she'd give him a new command, and rescind the last one, but she retired to sleep without addressing a single word to him, so he was left with the same order…and no idea what to say.

He wanted to give her good advice. He also needed to be honest, for a woman who could read his mind could surely spot a lie. Then again, was it not foolish to ask for advice on choosing one's life path from a man who had no memory of his own path, or any choice in it, and who knew even less about her past or the future she might wish to shape? He was her protector, not her adviser.

When he was sure she was safely asleep, Tor ascended to the rooftop, to pace it like a man driven mad with too many thoughts in his head. Over and over, he repeated what she'd told him in his head. The island, the cemetery, or the prison? Which should she wish to study most? And what…oh, horror of horrors, did he think?

The faint streaks of dawn lightened the sky, and he still had nothing to say.

Worse still…if Miss Kelly, infinitely more clever than he, could not make a choice, then how could he?

Then again, the worst she could do was send him back to the darkness. If he did not have the courage to answer her command, then he may as well return from whence he came.

If darkness would be his fate, whatever he chose, then he would at least not go as a coward.

Tor travelled to the wall of her bedchamber. He considered staying within the walls, so that all she would hear was his voice, as he had last night, but she deserved more than that. Besides, if she could see him hiding in the walls, then there was no hiding from her, anyway.

Tor stepped out of the plaster in the corner of her room, as far from the windows as he could get. He wrapped his wings about himself and ducked his head, in the deepest bow of respect he could manage.

"Miss Kelly, please forgive the lateness of my answer, but it is still morning, so I will venture to obey your command. You asked me to tell you what I think...and...I..."

His voice had died on him. Hell and damnation and that snotty superintendent's shrivelled left testicle…Tor cleared his throat and tried again.

"Miss Kelly, I think that you are far wiser than I shall ever be, and no one else is better placed than your own self to make important decisions about your future and happiness. My only desire is to see you safe and happy, and I will do everything within my power to help you to be both of those things. If there is anything I can do, you have but to ask, and it shall be done.

"But I think you know your own heart, and the island, the cemetery and the prison will not be enough to satisfy you, which is why you look elsewhere. It is my sincere hope that a new path may open its way to you, and that you will permit me to continue protecting you as you venture upon your chosen road."

Tor glanced up. Sunlight was already creeping through the curtains. He only had but a moment…

"I am honoured to be at your service," he said, before he was forced to flee.

THIRTEEN

Sleep did not come easy to Catena that night, and she woke before dawn, convinced the gargoyle had come down from the roof and was crouched in the corner of her bedroom, talking to her.

He'd said something about none of the projects being enough for her, and how he was honoured to be of service. She wished she could ask him to repeat it all, for it had sounded so flowery, but the corner where she'd thought he'd sat was empty now, lit by a stray ray of light from the rising sun.

There wasn't a gargoyle in her room – he was firmly stuck to the roof, where he belonged. Once she'd had breakfast, and a lot of coffee, then she could go up there and ask him to repeat himself, and feel like an idiot for dreaming about roof ornaments that talked.

Next thing she knew, she'd be talking to garden gnomes. Hmm, best to avoid Bunnings for a bit, then, in case she was tempted to try.

Luckily, there weren't any in the library, where she'd be working for most of today. As long as she was awake enough to walk there, which would require…coffee.

She padded downstairs to the kitchen, where she managed to slot a pod into the coffee machine and fix herself a bowl of cereal, without giving in to the temptation that was the box of cannoli. But only just.

Some time later, showered, dressed (and double checked to make sure she hadn't stuck her shirt on inside out or anything), she brewed a second cup of coffee. She reached for her travel mug to pour it into for the walk to work, then checked the time and realised that waking up early had its advantages – she had time to drink this before she needed to leave for work.

Her cup was empty too soon, though she didn't feel any more alert than when she'd woken up. Oh, well – it should be quiet in the library today, so no one would notice if she was a little slower and sleepier than usual. Unless she fell asleep at the enquiries desk, of course…now that would be embarrassing!

No, she'd never be that unprofessional. Instead, she'd do her job, and forget about research proposals for a few days. The dream gargoyle…okay, probably her own subconscious…was right, and waiting was the way to go. She'd get the proposal in at the last minute, anyway, just like everyone else.

Right. Shoes. Wallet. Phone. Keys…where were her…oh, there they were, under her sunglasses. She might need those, because it was sunny today, even if it was winter.

As ready as she'd ever be, Catena headed out the door for what she hoped would be a good day.

FOURTEEN

"Miss!"

"Are you the Moth Man?"

"Are you dating the Moth Man?"

"Miss! Miss! Do you know the Moth Man?"

Catena hadn't even closed the outer door before they converged, coming at her from all directions with cameras and microphones and phones and so much shouting…

So she did what she always did when

someone started shouting at her. She bolted.

67

FIFTEEN

She extended her hand, palm out, stopping him. "No."

The thinnest stone veneer stood between him and the mob who surrounded her. The mob he needed to protect her from. Who was Miss Kelly to say NO when protecting her was his purpose?

Yet he obeyed, like the lowliest slave, for he knew what might happen if he did not. The whip of her words, sending him back into the darkness, where he could not protect her at all.

The sun bathed the crowd then, as if it had lain in wait behind a cloud, ready to catch him in its grasp and turn him into a statue, if he had but ignored her command and waded into the fray. Light that haloed the mob who were anything but angels.

Except the escaping scholar who had refused his help, running down the street with the morning light on her back. Safe, for none of them had given chase.

Not like the man that first night, when she'd asked for his help, not said NO.

He could not say no. He was called to protect, to defend, to work. If he said no, then he would never be free.

Free to choose, to refuse what he did not want…

Had he ever truly been free? Would he?

The stone surrounding him weighed heavily on his shoulders. Tonnes of limestone filled with tiny shells that had once been free to swim in the sea, now as trapped as he was.

Yet it still wasn't as heavy as chains. If he was free to choose, he would always choose stone over steel.

Catena was a scholar, so much more educated than he would ever be. Perhaps she was right to say no, for she knew more than he did. He could see she was safe, slowing to a walk as she rounded the corner.

SIXTEEN

By the time she rounded the second corner, the journalists or whatever they were, had given up on their pursuit, and Catena dared to slow down again and catch her breath. She'd emerged relatively unscathed from the scrum, but her travel cup of coffee was another matter. Catena sighed. She'd have to head to the staff room to make another cup, because the dregs of this one weren't worth drinking.

Callie, the Latin lecturer, was already in there.

"Good morning," Catena greeted her.

Callie held up her hand. "Before you ask, let me stop you right there. No, I don't know anything about Moth Men. No, I didn't see it last night, and no, there are no historical accounts of anything even faintly resembling a Moth Man in any part of my archives, because a Moth Man is an urban myth, based on a hoax staged in some small town in America. There is no Moth Man, there never has been a Moth Man, and there never will be, because they do not exist!"

Had Callie seen the media crew outside her house? No, surely not. Evidently she'd been bitten by the same bug as those reporters.

"What is a Moth Man, and why is everyone so interested in him, all of a sudden?" Catena asked, peeling off the lid of her cup and pouring what remained down the drain. Ugh, there was coffee everywhere - she'd have to wash and dry it before she dared take it into the library.

Callie waved her hand in dismissal. "It's a myth. The only reason everyone's talking about it is because someone dressed up in a bad Batman costume, filmed it, stuck in some special effects, and then posted the video online, where it's gone viral. Even the news websites have picked it up, because it's the second monster sighting in Fremantle in the last month, or at least that's what they're saying." She snorted. "As if zombies were real, either."

Catena wondered if she was still dreaming, because none of this made sense. "There's a zombie in Fremantle?"

"Of course there isn't. Not even a fake one – someone would have caught it on camera if there was. No, it was a prank pulled by some high school kids, I'm sure of it. Someone dug up an old grave at the first Fremantle cemetery, left some hand and foot prints in the soft soil around it. Like a zombie had risen or something, or at least that's the story the kids told, when they got to the police station. Something about a man shambling away. If you ask me, they probably disturbed some homeless man, sleeping in the bushes. Serves them right."

Zombies and Moth Men. In Fremantle. What next? Catena managed a weak smile. "Who'd have pegged Fremantle as Monster Central? In the movies, it's usually some American small town, or the seedy parts of one of their cities. What next? Vampires? Demons? The Winchester brothers?"

Callie shook her head. "While I wouldn't say no to a visit from Sam and Dean, it's got to be a stunt. Monsters don't exist. At least, not the supernatural kind. Just people who do horrible things." She shrugged. "Watch the video for yourself. Search up the Fremantle Moth Man — you'll find it. See how fake it looks. We won't be hoping for a visit from the Winchesters or whatever their real life equivalent is any time soon."

If only those reporters this morning had

been as sensible as Callie. Ah, but it was all about sensation, wasn't it? Chasing a story…

Speaking of stories, she'd have to make one up if she didn't get to the library right away to explain why it hadn't opened on time.

She could watch the video at her desk, when she had a moment. Then she'd know what a Moth Man was, and hopefully how to avoid anything to do with them ever again.

The morning passed in a blur of enquiries, most of them students looking for…yes, information on the Moth Man. It seemed like, the moment they finished their exams, they felt like the most appropriate thing to do was go chasing conspiracy theory monsters. She couldn't recall ever doing that after an exam. No, her post exam celebrations had usually involved alcohol, not more research.

The library cleared out shortly after lunch, though, and that's when she dared to search for the silly video. She had to play it muted, or risk disturbing someone still studying, but the images were enough.

It looked like the video had been filmed from one of the upstairs windows across the street from her house, for she recognised the downstairs shops clearly enough. The Moth Man – who did look like Batman, she had to admit – spread his cape or wings or whatever he wore wide, and she watched herself run straight into him. The man chasing her threw his arms up in the air, skidded to a stop, then raced back the way he'd come, and Batman or Moth Man or whoever he was just sort of spun toward the doorway, then disappeared. She had to watch it several times, but there was no mistaking the sweater she'd been wearing on Friday night, or how well the video tallied with her own memories. She'd run into someone and woken up in her own bed. She almost wished the video had been longer, showing the moments after her memories went blank, but that's all there was. She should be thankful it didn't show her face, or the reporters this morning wouldn't have let her go so easily.

Oh, damn, the reporters – how long would

they wait outside her house? Surely not all day. If they were waiting for her when she came home…

"Um, 'scuse me. I was wondering if you could tell me where I could find books about the Moth Man?"

Catena looked up from her screen and into the bloodshot eyes of a student who'd definitely pulled an all-nighter before today's exam. If he only had the presence of mind to pull out his phone and spend five minutes searching the internet… She sighed and gave him her polite smile for stupid children. "We don't have any fiction in this library. Perhaps the City of Fremantle's public library can help you. They're up near the Town Hall."

She'd been saying the same thing all day, but this guy seemed more crestfallen than the rest. "Oh. 'Kay then. I guess I'll try there, then." He shambled off. Catena sincerely hoped he fell into bed for a decent night's sleep before heading to any other libraries.

Now she had to hope there wouldn't be

anyone in the way when she went home to her bed tonight.

SEVENTEEN

All day, Tor stewed about his failure. What he should or should not have done. Even as he thought of questioning Miss Kelly, he heard the clink of chains echoing in his mind. He knew the weight of them on his wrists, his ankles, the tight canvas cuffs strapped around him to stop the chafing but it was never enough, worn thin from use.

It was those ghostly chains that kept him

within the walls, obedient to her will, until the sun sank beneath the horizon and finally, finally, far too long after that…she returned.

Light clicked on in the kitchen, her things clattering to the bench. Light that drew him like a moth to the warmth of her flame. Not that she had any flames or fires in this house. It was quite strange, really. She had fireplaces, but no grates and no fires were laid. He knew they had to keep warm somehow, and then there was cooking. Miss Kelly did not look undernourished, so there must be some way she cooked her meals. Or maybe someone else cooked for her, so she had no need to risk a fire in her house.

And yet…no one had come to visit or bring her meals the whole time he'd been guarding her. So that could not be it.

He'd simply have to ask her. And hope that she would not punish him for questioning her.

He offered up a silent prayer that Miss Kelly would be both merciful and forthcoming, then took a deep breath and stepped forth into her presence.

EIGHTEEN

She stayed on the other side of the street on her walk home. If the press crew were still camped outside her front door, she'd see them in time to detour around the corner and sneak in the back door.

Catena found a crowd, all right, but they weren't at her house. Instead, they were milling around outside the café over the road from her. The café with upstairs windows set at just the right angle for that video to have been taken from one of them…

She scrutinised the crowd. Was the person who'd filmed that video standing among them?

It could be any of them, she decided. Most of them had their phones out, while clutching a coffee in their other hand, all avidly watching the footpath in front of her house.

Catena sighed. The back door it'd have to be, then.

Around the corner, through the tiny carpark courtyard, and up the steps to the back door. A quick twist of the key and she was in, clicking the door closed behind her as she prayed no one had noticed. Past the storage room doors, which she'd never opened, and up another short flight of steps to the main entrance hall. Then up the grand staircase, a little more unlocking, and she was safely inside her apartment.

Her next mission: to work out what to have for dinner. She had a hankering for pasta, but she couldn't remember if she'd left the mince for the bolognese sauce in the fridge or the freezer. Damn, it looked like she'd frozen it in. Well, she had mushrooms and bacon. Together with a creamy sauce, those would work well with pasta.

She seized the packet of bacon and carried it over to the bench.

Or at least she tried to. The packet dropped from her nerveless fingers about halfway there, when she caught sight of the man standing in her kitchen.

The bloody Moth Man from the video, no less.

Catena didn't think. She grabbed the chef's knife from the knife block, pointed it firmly in his direction and said, "Who the fuck are you and what the fuck are you doing in my house?"

She was rather proud of how her voice didn't shake, though her knees definitely wanted to.

The man – for of course he was just a man, moth men didn't actually exist – was massive. Built like the proverbial brick dunny, especially when he folded his arms like that, making the muscles bulge.

He was so wide she almost didn't see his wings at first, jutting out from his shoulders but folded back behind him like a long, leather trenchcoat. Except it wasn't a trenchcoat, because his brawny shoulders were as bare as the rest of him. No shirt, no…holy hell, he needed to put some pants over that thing, because he was definitely proportionate in all the right places.

"Miss Kelly?"

She jerked her gaze up from his groin to his face.

"Miss Kelly, I'm Tor, your sworn protector. You summoned me."

No, she'd definitely remember summoning…a naked man in her kitchen. One with fake wings strapped to his back somehow, because those couldn't possibly be real. Moth men didn't exist.

"That's not possible," she said, trying and failing to sound like she believed her own words. Because there was no way she was hallucinating Hercules here in her kitchen.

"I assure you it is. You summoned me the other night to rescue you from your pursuer, and I did. I am here to protect you. That is my purpose."

He really was the Moth Man, or at least the man in the video. She had to get a closer look at his wings. Then she'd know they were fake.

"Turn around. Show me your wings," she ordered.

He inclined his head, then did as she asked.

At a quick glance, she might have mistaken his folded wings for a trenchcoat, but then he began to extend them, like a giant bat spread from one wall to the other, all the way across her kitchen. Massive wingspan, which she imagined he'd need in order to lift all those muscles off the ground.

Yep, that back. All those bunched up muscles, supporting the weight of his wings, right down to his dimples. Well, she'd never understood how someone's arse could look like a perfect peach, but there was the evidence, right there. Two gorgeous globes that she really shouldn't be staring at. Dean Winchester would die of envy, if he saw these.

"Would you like to touch them?"

Yes. Actually, she'd like to reach out and squeeze, to see if those butt cheeks felt as luscious as they looked.

Catena cleared her throat, trying to break herself out of this lust-filled trance. She was not considering groping the stranger in her kitchen. Not at all.

"No, I…you can put them away, thanks. Now tell me how you got in here." She folded her arms across her chest, in a desperate attempt to stop herself from reaching for the strange man.

"Why, the same way I did when I saved you the other night. Through the walls."

Through the walls. That made no sense. Wait, ghosts could walk through walls. Well, if they existed, which she wasn't exactly sure about.

"Are you a ghost?" she demanded.

Tor laughed softly. "No, Miss Kelly. I'm as corporeal as you. See?" He extended his hand toward her, palm up.

She brandished the knife. "You stay back. Don't come any closer." Yet her free hand reached out, yearning to take his, or at least to touch. She touched the tip of her index finger to his palm. Warm and hard, just as she expected him to feel. Swallowing, she stroked her hand across his, just the once. His skin was rough, like he didn't moisturise much. Or maybe it was callouses, from working for a living, because he had to do something strenuous all day to have muscles like that.

"You can put down the knife, Miss Kelly. I assure you I am here to protect you, and I mean you no harm. If you try to cut me, you would only blunt the blade, for my skin is not as fragile as yours." He reached out and ran his hand along the blade, then showed her his palm. No blood, though there was a little dust. As if the blade had scraped... "I'm made of living stone, the better to protect you."

"What are you?"

If he said he was the Moth Man, she was going to throw the knife at him, Catena decided.

"I'm a gargoyle, your stone protector."

Catena burst out laughing. Of all the things he could have said, this was the last one she'd expected.

"My gargoyle is up on the roof. He's round and grotesque, not built like…" She gestured at the length of his body, only to find herself staring again. "Damn it, could you put on some pants already?"

Tor's eyes followed her gaze. "Oh, please forgive me, Miss Kelly." He brought one of his wings around, so that it covered his groin. "If you provide me with the appropriate livery, I would be only too happy to wear it."

Livery? Wasn't that something to do with horses and stables? Or servants? Yeah, it was a uniform, wasn't it? That rich people made their servants wear and they had the same mark on all their stuff?

Not people like her who scraped by on a part-time librarian's wage or the pittance of a PhD scholarship, if she could actually secure one.

"You must have made a mistake. You can't be my protector. I'm not the sort of person who needs a protector. I'm nobody!" she insisted.

Tor shook his head. "Miss Kelly, if I were not your protector, you could not have summoned me. Therefore, when you called for me, and I came, I became your protector. You are not nobody. In fact, you are so important, that protecting you is my sole purpose. It was the reason I became a gargoyle in the first place. I live only to serve you." He bowed deeply, like he'd stepped out of a regency romance and not the wall, like he'd said.

How did the wall thing work, then? "Fine. You're my protector, then, I guess. Whatever that means. But…how do you walk through walls?"

"I am living stone, and your walls are also made of stone. I simply slip through them like a fish swimming through water." He turned, flashing that glorious butt again, before he stepped into the wall and disappeared. A moment later, his foot poked out, then a leg, then…ohGodohGod…DON'T STARE AT HIS GROIN…ohGod…before Tor stood before her again, looking pretty pleased with himself.

It had to be some sort of trick. One that involved mirrors or something. Catena wanted to believe it was a trick, but this was her kitchen. The one with solid limestone walls that had stood for more than a century. She could not deny she'd seen him walk into that stone wall, and then step out again. But if he had, then he wasn't just a man. He was more than that, something supernatural, which couldn't possibly exist.

Her mind whirled furiously, trying to put the pieces together. Worse, she wanted to believe. "So, on Friday night, when you first appeared, and you grabbed me, you took me inside the walls, all the way up to my bedroom?"

Tor frowned. "Yes. I must apologise, for it was the first time I had tried travelling through stone with someone, and I did not realise you would not be able to breathe. It was only when we reached your bedchamber that I realised you had swooned. I did not know where you kept your smelling salts, so I waited until you awoke, presented my apologies, and returned to the walls, as it was near dawn. Do you not remember?"

Vaguely, but she'd thought he was a dream. God, had he been watching her sleep? Worse than the vampire in Twilight. And vampires couldn't hide in the walls. He could have been watching her in the shower or…wait, what had he just said?

"Dawn? What's the deal with dawn? You're not a vampire, are you?" she asked.

"I'm not sure what a vampire is, Miss Kelly."

Catena smothered a laugh. Fancy that. A supernatural creature who didn't know everything about all the other kinds of monsters. Or maybe that was just because vampires didn't exist and Tor…did.

"Uh, blood sucking, pale skin, afraid of sunlight, can't enter your house unless you invite them…" Well, that definitely ruled Tor out, then.

Tor chuckled, a rumbling sound that did peculiar things to Catena's belly. "It sounds like a villain in a gothic novel. Or so I believe, for I haven't read many myself. Perhaps you have been doing too much reading, Miss Kelly, to imagine such wild things."

Like a ripped, naked gargoyle in her kitchen. She wanted this all to be a figment of her imagination. Then again, maybe she didn't. If she could maybe make sense of this in her head, make sense of him, she'd get to stare at him for a few minutes more before he poofed out of existence, like all good hallucinations.

"But the dawn thing?" she prompted.

"Like your...fan-pyre, I do have a weakness when it comes to sunlight. In the sun's rays, I turn to stone, much like the statue on your rooftop."

Horror overcame Catena. "You mean the statue is alive, trapped there in stone?"

"No, the statue on your roof is no more than a statue. Ordinary stone. I can slip inside of it as easily as I do the walls. If I were to sit on your roof at dawn, you would find a statue much like I am now."

Muscles. Wings. No pants, so the whole world would see his massive...

"Forever?"

"No, of course not. Just until the sun went down, and then I would be myself again. I would still see and hear everything around me, just as I do when I'm within the walls, I just couldn't move while I was still in sunlight. Which is why I spend my days sheltering within your walls."

She wasn't sure why his words gave her a warm feeling inside, but somehow they did.

Hadn't Maria said something similar on her visit yesterday? She'd talked about the gargoyle in the house, too…had she meant Tor, and not the statue on the roof?

If Maria knew about him, then maybe he really was the protector he'd said he was. Which meant he belonged here more than Catena did.

"How long have you been here, Tor?" she asked.

He lifted his shoulders in a massive shrug. "I do not know. I've been in the darkness, awaiting your call."

Poor man. No, poor gargoyle. "What's your last memory, before…darkness?"

A wince of pain creased his expression for only a moment, before it was gone. "I have no memories before the darkness. Then I heard your call, and emerged into the light. A strange light, burning without fire. Most strange."

So Tor was from a time before electric lights. Maybe he was as old as the house, or even older.

"Miss Kelly, may I presume to ask you a question?" he asked.

It'd been a long time since she'd learned about light globes and electricity at school, but she figured she could remember enough to talk him through it. If that failed, she'd pull out her phone and show him a picture. "Sure," she said.

NINETEEN

Tor took a deep breath. "Miss Kelly, I am your protector. It's my sole purpose to see that you don't come to harm. So why did you not permit me to help you against that mob this morning? Did you not think me capable of doing so?"

Catena blew out a breath of her own. She'd been ready to talk about magnets and electrons, but talking a guy down from performance anxiety was much more her style. She beamed at him. "Tor, it only takes one look at you to tell me that you're the best protector anyone could have. I mean, that guy on Friday night only had to look at you before he ran away. If I had to imagine the best bodyguard in the world, you'd be the super ultra mega deluxe version with all the extras only world leaders can afford."

"Then why did you not allow me to protect you this morning?"

"I didn't even know you were here, or that you would protect me. Come to think of it, the sun was well and truly up this morning. Wouldn't you have just turned to stone anyway?"

Tor drew himself up. "That would not have stopped me. I would have driven them off from the shadows in the doorway, letting loose an almighty roar to terrify them, before appearing in their midst. By the time I turned to stone, they would have all fled in horror."

Leaving a naked gargoyle statue in the

doorway for everyone to photograph, bringing even more people tomorrow.

Horror, all right. But she lived here – she couldn't flee from it.

She swallowed. "You can't go out the front door. Not when there are people out there. They'll see you, and then they'll film you and then they'll never leave us alone."

"Of course they will. Am I not terrifying?"

"Well, yes, but…"

"Am I not a capable protector?"

She couldn't deny that, either.

"Of course you are, Tor, but they're not here to attack me. They're here to see you, and the more they see of you, the more they'll come here."

"This is lunacy. What manner of person likes to be terrified, likes it so much that they return for more?"

Millions of horror movie fans, not to mention readers of gothic novels. Even she'd read a few Stephen King books, until the sleepless nights and nightmares had gotten to her and she'd had to stop. In fact, the only horror film she'd ever managed to watch a second time was The Mummy, for obvious reasons.

"A lot of people. Probably crazy people, yes, but…they find it entertaining. Look, if you stick around, I'll watch The Mummy with you, and you can see what I mean. But right now…there's a café full of people over the road, dying for a glimpse of you, or a picture on their phone. And if they get so much as a single, blurry picture, tomorrow there will be two or three or even ten times as many people. So you have to stay inside, where they can't see you."

Tor blinked. Maybe it was a lot to take in for a gargoyle who'd only been awake for three days, after sleeping who knew how long. "Miss Kelly, I find this very hard to believe, though I do not believe you would lie to me. I must observe these lunatics for myself, for if they are a danger to you, I cannot allow them to remain. Even if they make pictures of me."

Catena buried her face in her hands. "Tor, you can't…look, I'll take you up to the roof. Hopefully they won't see us up there, and I can show you what I mean. C'mon." This time, she held out her hand, and Tor took it. His grip was warm and gentle, as if he feared he might break her fingers if he held on too tight. He probably could, too.

She led him upstairs, then up through the French doors to the rooftop.

The moment the wind hit her, straight off the sea and likely fresh from the South Pole, she wished she'd thought to bring a coat. Oh well, they'd only be out here a moment.

Then Tor emerged, and his spread wings blocked the breeze.

Catena wanted to turn around and hug him, but she managed to stifle the urge, and led him to the edge of the rooftop instead. Ducking down behind the gargoyle statue, she could feel the heat of Tor crouching in close behind her.

"Look, there's the café across the road from

us," she said, pointing at the Shut Up Café. She'd never noticed the name before. Evidently, the noisy patrons outside hadn't, either. "Everyone out there is watching the entrance to our place, where you first appeared on Friday night. They're watching and waiting, hoping to take a picture."

"They don't look like lunatics, but what are they all doing, crowding around outside, when there are tables and chairs to spare inside? Perhaps they are crazy, after all."

"There's a better view outside. With all the bright light inside, you can't see what's going on in the shadows across the street, which is what they really want to see. Besides, you can't get a good picture through glass." She wondered if she'd have to explain photography to Tor, too.

"I see." He peered out at them, as if searching for something that he couldn't find. "What I don't see is anyone about to make a picture. Not a sketchpad or pencil among them. I can't imagine how a picture could be a bad thing. It takes considerable skill and practice to become a good artist, so I don't imagine one in a thousand could create a passable picture that looks anything like me. Or why I should care if they did."

Catena could feel a headache coming on. How could she explain what a viral video was to a man who didn't understand the existence of phone cameras? She'd have to try. Because between Tor's size and his ability to walk through walls, she hadn't a hope of stopping him if he wanted to go outside and confront the café patrons.

She took a deep breath. "Okay, you see those things in their hands? Those rectangular things?" She waited for Tor to nod, then pulled her own phone out of her pocket. "This is mine. It's a communications device that allows me to take pictures and share them with everyone in the world. Through a thing called the internet…a sort of invisible network that goes right round the world."

To her surprise, she found Tor nodding.

"We called it the aether."

That sounded like something to do with alchemy, or weird science theories that got debunked centuries ago. "Uh, yeah, something like that. Anyway, it can instantly take a picture of anything it sees, and share it."

"A machine does not have eyes. It cannot see anything."

No, she was not going to try to explain robotics to him. "Will you just trust me for a moment, okay? It's a lens, not an eye, but the principle is the same. Here, look at this, and smile." She pointed at the lens on her phone, waited for him to stare at it, then snapped a picture. Definitely not a vampire. She flipped her phone around to show him. "See?"

He peered at it. "That looks like me, but…how…"

Explaining camera phones was way beyond her level of expertise. Plus she was hungry, damn it.

Catena threw an arm around Tor's shoulders, leaned back, and held up her phone.

She thumbed the screen to use the front camera instead of the rear one. "Smile for your first selfie!"

"Hey, that's me!"

She snapped a shot of his smile of wonderment, and had to admit she didn't look too bad in the photo, either. A pity she'd never be able to show it to anyone, because no one would believe gargoyles existed.

She'd still save it, though, so that she could take it out and look at it to remind herself that she hadn't dreamed this.

Wait, what was that poking her in the back? All hard and pokey and…oh God, was that his…?

"Please forgive me, Miss Kelly, I seem to have gotten tangled up in your…in your clothing…"

He shifted, and then he was heating the pocket of her sweater instead.

"We need to get you some pants," she bit out, closing her eyes so she wouldn't see anything as he extracted his wayward appendage.

Of course, she couldn't help peeking a little. If anything, he'd actually gotten bigger and harder. Had their little hug given the gargoyle a hard-on? It seemed that it had. Huh.

When he'd managed to disentangle them and backed up enough for her to get past, she led the way back inside, to the laundry, where Maria had kept all her dig clothes.

"My godmother used to keep a collection of men's cargo pants in here, to wear when she went out to archaeological sites. You should be able to find something to fit you in one of these drawers." She waved at them. "When you're decent, you can come find me in the kitchen, where I'll be making dinner."

She marched off, determined not to think about his monster dick and what it might feel like somewhere more personal than her pocket. Definitely not thinking about sleeping with the gargoyle, riding him hard for half the night. Nope. Not at all.

Would it even fit?

Nope. Not thinking about it at all…

TWENTY

Tor was surprised to find she did indeed have some pants that fitted him. They were made from a heavy, cream-coloured cotton and fastened at the waist with a length of cord, cunningly hidden on the inside. So much finer than the scratchy fustian he'd been forced to wear before. These suited him better than any livery. He must thank Miss Kelly.

Almost without thinking, he slipped

through the walls to arrive in the kitchen, where he found her stirring something in a pan on the stove. A blue flame did indeed appear underneath the pan, solving the mystery of her meals.

"Oh, good, you found some," she said.

Tor glanced down. It appeared his pants could travel through walls, as well, or at least while he was wearing them. Good. For if a single touch from Miss Kelly could arouse him so powerfully…he was her protector, not her paramour, even if someone like Miss Kelly would consider taking a lover. She'd never choose someone as lowly as him. Best he remember that.

"I'm making enough for two, in case you want some. I usually make extra, so I can have leftovers for later," Miss Kelly said, still stirring. The appetising aroma of bacon rose up to assail his nose.

Damn, he hadn't eaten bacon in…no, he could not remember that, either.

"I have no need for sustenance, being made

of stone," he said sadly. He'd make an exception for that bacon, though.

"You don't have to eat? Not ever? I can't imagine what that must be like. To never taste bacon…"

Tor swallowed. "I remember what bacon tastes like, so I must have eaten it once. Not that I remember when."

She stared at him. "So you haven't always been a gargoyle, then?"

He shrugged. "I can remember nothing of my past."

Miss Kelly had a deft hand with a knife, as she alternated between slicing mushrooms and stirring the bacon.

"You sound Scottish. Is that where you're from? Do you remember anything from there?" she pressed.

Tor racked his brain, but came up with nothing. "Wherever I came from, this is my home now." These words rang with truth. Memory twinged, just the tiniest pang of yearning, before it was gone, too quickly to grasp. "I have no memory of anywhere else."

"Is that a gargoyle thing? Are there any other gargoyle things I should know, like your issue with sunlight?"

Tor pondered. "I don't know. I've never met another gargoyle. I only know that I am bound to serve, and protect, and I will."

Miss Kelly scraped the mushrooms into the pan. "That doesn't seem fair. You do all the hard work, serving and protecting, and sleeping in the darkness for who knows how long, waiting to be called, and what do you get out of it? Sounds like slavery to me, and that was abolished a long time ago."

What could he say? "It is my purpose."

"Protecting me sounds like a pretty shitty purpose in life. Isn't there anything you want to do?"

There was something, dancing on the tip of his tongue, tingling at his fingertips, just out of reach, but whatever it was, Tor could not grasp it. "Perhaps there was once, but not any more. I am what I am, and no more." He coughed.

"If you'll forgive my impertinence, I wish to ask another question."

"Just ask, Tor. I've already forgiven you for accidentally sticking your dick in my pocket, so let's just assume I'm okay with a bit of impertinence, as long as you're wearing pants, okay?"

Tor almost choked. "Miss Kelly, are all lady scholars of this time as outspoken as you, or is it just your tongue that is unusually salty?"

Miss Kelly laughed. "I don't know what time you're actually from, but I'm beginning to think it's a lot different to this one. No one's ever called me a lady scholar before, though I admit I kind of like it. And I'm probably no more salty than most of the women I know. Oh, and drop the Miss Kelly thing. My name is Catena, or occasionally Cat. This is Australia. We don't do honorifics unless we really hate someone, or maybe if they're the prime minister. Come to think of it…yeah, definitely the prime minister, on both counts, at the moment. We've got a real dickhead in office right now."

"You're…not what I expected."

She snorted. "Well, you're definitely not what I expected. If anyone had told me I'd have a conversation with a gargoyle in my kitchen, I wouldn't have believed them. Yet, here we are."

She busied herself about the kitchen, putting things in pots, then pouring them out again, until she filled a bowl with long, stringy things before spooning the mushroom and bacon sauce over the top.

"I feel bad eating in front of you, when you can't and all. Is there anything I can get you?" she said.

It sounded silly, but something made him say it anyway. "May I…just sit near you, so that I might smell it? Even if I can't eat it, I can enjoy the scent, for it smells quite delicious."

She grinned. "I can do you one better. I'll put all the leftovers in a box, then set it in front of you, so you can sniff to your heart's content while it cools off."

She might have a salty tongue, but she certainly was remarkably thoughtful.

"Thank you, Miss…Catena."

"And when we're done, we're going to watch *The Mummy*."

"Aren't those from Egypt?" he ventured.

Her smile widened. "Indeed they are. This movie's set there. It's about a lady scholar and librarian, and an archaeological dig in Egypt where they dig up something they shouldn't…"

"It sounds like a gothic novel."

"Does it? For all that you said you didn't read them, you sure know a lot about them. Maybe you've read more than you're willing to admit."

Try as he might, Tor could not remember reading much of anything, but he followed Catena into the next room to see whatever it was she wanted to watch.

TWENTY-ONE

The moving picture with sound, appearing on the black screen on the wall, were entirely new to Tor. He might not remember much about his past, but it definitely hadn't included movies. Unlike Catena, who had seen this one so many times, she knew many of the lines by heart.

In fact, she'd fallen asleep before he'd found out how the story ended, curling up on her side on her couch while he'd watched every moment.

Now, he was torn. As her protector, surely it fell to him to make sure she was warm and comfortable as she slept, instead of all cramped on the couch, when she had a large, fine bed in another room. Yet he didn't want to wake her, and while he was more than up to the task of carrying her to her bedchamber, now he knew his body's reaction to touching her, he wasn't sure if he should.

Well, it wasn't like he was going to ravish her as she slept, he reasoned, no matter how much certain parts of his body relished that idea. His head ruled here, and he would protect her from any and all threats, including the wicked parts of himself. He couldn't remember the last time a woman had made him feel like this – after all, he couldn't remember much of anything – but he suspected there was something special about Catena that made her utterly unique. Why else was he charged with protecting her?

Carefully, he scooped her up from the couch, shifting her weight until her head rested snugly against his chest. Her hair smelled like exotic fruit, sweet and sensual all at the same time. He breathed deep, savouring it as surely as he had the bacon smells in her kitchen.

"I'm…a librarian," she mumbled, rubbing her face against his chest.

Tor smiled. Another line from the movie that she knew by heart. She was a strange woman in an even stranger world.

Carrying his precious cargo, he remembered not to slip through the walls, and instead trudged through doorways and passages to reach her room, where he laid her on the bed. She'd made a point of going off to change into her night clothes, so he knew she wouldn't mind if he peeled back the coverlet, and pulled it over her.

Then he was at a loss for what to do. He could watch over her as she slept, he supposed, but the café across the road had since closed, and most of the people outside had dispersed. All of Catena's doors were locked, so there were no threats to her, inside or outside, for him to watch for.

Watching her sleep made his mouth inexplicably dry, or dryer than usual, given he was made of stone. He cast his eyes about her room, looking for something, anything, that might pose a threat to her that he might deal with.

Wait, was that a crack in the wall, up near the ceiling?

Indeed it was. A hairline crack in the plaster, but as he delved deeper, he found the crack originated in the limestone wall itself. Oh, that would never do. Her house could not be permitted to fall down around her while she slept.

He'd seen some construction materials downstairs, where someone was rebuilding the road during the day, so he borrowed a little of the limestone and a lot of other things, and set to work.

Some time during the night, as he worked to

fill the gaps in the crumbling limestone, cursing the poor quality of the stuff, he had a flash of memory, his own voice cursing the stone, as bright sunlight beat down on him and the tall, white wall.

"If you don't build buttresses, one good gust of wind'll send the walls toppling," he heard himself say.

"If we build buttresses, the prisoners will climb up them and escape. You do as you're told. The engineers know what they're doing."

"They don't if they're not building buttresses."

"You do as you're told, convict, or it'll be manacles and motley for you."

"It'll be manacles and motley for everyone, for when these un-buttressed walls come down, everyone will escape."

Pain turned the memory blinding white, and Tor found himself blinking at Catena's wall again, though he still felt the sharp sting of the lash on his back and the weight of the manacles at his ankles.

Of all the memories of his past, this was one he'd have happily forgotten. Back to work, then, for working stone always made him forget anything but the wall in front of him.

He might not remember much, but he knew how to build and maintain a wall that would last for centuries. Maybe it was a gargoyle thing, or maybe it was something he remembered from before, but it didn't matter.

By the time the sun rose, he'd carefully patched every wall in her bedroom, and the kitchen, too. Tomorrow night, he'd do more, until Catena's house was as sound and secure as any lady's castle. His salt-tongued lady scholar deserved no less.

TWENTY-TWO

Catena woke when the sun rose, to find she was securely tucked into her own bed and Tor was nowhere to be seen. The TV was still on in the lounge room – she'd evidently fallen asleep before the movie ended, and Tor hadn't known how to turn it off. Something else she'd have to explain to her new gargoyle roommate.

Who needed more than one pair of Maria's old cargo pants to wear.

Catena knew nothing about men's clothes or sizing, but she knew someone who did: Tayla, who owned the menswear store downstairs. If Catena covered Tor's wings with a big coat, maybe she'd be able to bring him down to try things on. Oh, but he couldn't come out during the day, so it'd have to be at night.

"Good morning!" Catena called as she spotted Tayla unlocking her door.

"Morning. It's too cold to be good. Can't wait until it's summer again," Tayla said. "I'll be ordering the summer stock today, and the spring collection's just come in."

"But it's only June!"

"That's the way the fashion industry works. Always a few months ahead of where anyone else has any sense being," Tayla said.

"Oh, speaking of strange timing…a colleague of mine has just flown in, and none of his luggage arrived with him, so he's got nothing to wear, and he's working at the university tomorrow. Is there any chance you could stay open a little later tonight, so I could bring him in to buy a few things to tide him over? He's asleep now – he says he can't sleep on planes and time zones are a killer – but when he wakes up later…" Catena drifted off hopefully.

Tayla shook her head. "Sorry, darl, my son's got a dentist appointment this afternoon, so I have to close early as it is. Tell you what, though. You know where the spare keys are. Bring him in when he wakes up and try things on anyway. Leave the tags on the cash register, and I'll bill you tomorrow morning for them. Oh, and the stocktake sale starts tomorrow, where I'll discount all the remaining winter stock to half price. The sale rack will be here in the back. Check that first – he'll want winter clothes if it's for this week."

Catena thanked her profusely. She checked the footpath outside, which was miraculously free of reporters, and headed out to work for the day.

TWENTY-THREE

A scratchy voice found him within the walls of Catena's house, while the wan winter sunlight kept him captive.

"I can help you escape," the voice said. "Meet me here after dark. You can help me, and I can help you."

Tor didn't trust that voice, not one bit, and he'd wanted to ignore it.

Wanted to forget the florid face of the

butcher, his cleaver still dripping from the sheep he'd just slaughtered, as he nodded knowingly at Tor's chains.

"I know you want to escape. Come here after dark, and I'll help you."

Then all was dark, except the striations of the stone. Calming and familiar, cold and hard, but inside he was screaming at himself not to trust the butcher.

Yet somehow, he'd silenced the screaming, or it had been drowned out by the clink of his chains and the agony of his lashed back, and he'd been seduced by that scratchy whisper.

The same voice that urged him to protect her.

Of course he'd protect Catena. How could he not? And yet when the scratchy voice ordered him to do it, he longed to rebel. To resist.

But how could he possibly resist her?

TWENTY-FOUR

"Can we watch more of those moving pictures?" Tor asked before Catena had even put her keys down.

She had to laugh. He'd known about TV for a day, and already he was addicted to it. "Sure. Actually, there's blockout blinds in the lounge room. If you keep those down during the day, it should keep enough sunlight out of the room for you to stay in there and watch whatever you want to while I'm at work. I'll show you how to use everything tonight, before I go to bed. But first I need to have dinner, and you need more than one pair of pants, so come with me. My friend owns the men's clothing store downstairs, and I'm hoping she might have something that will fit you. Pants, shirts…underwear, even. Oh, and a winter coat. You make me cold just looking at you, wandering around without a shirt."

Actually, that shivery feeling she felt every time she stared at his chest had very little to do with cold, but she was hardly going to tell him the truth. He was her protector, as he'd said so many times last night, which sort of made him her employee or subordinate or something, and she knew how wrong it was to molest the people who worked for you. Even if she wasn't paying him, or asking him to protect her, or however it worked.

So he needed shirts, and more pants and a whole lot of underwear.

It was dark in the foyer, and dark in Tayla's

shop. The winter sales racks were right in the back, as promised, beside the change rooms, and out of view of the street. So even if the café patrons were looking for the Moth Man tonight, they wouldn't see Tor as he tried on clothes.

She thought shirts would be the easiest, so she started with those. Of course, she hadn't considered Tor's wings, which strained at the fabric of even the biggest shirts and stuck out the bottom.

She sighed, resigned to staring at his chest muscles and abs for the foreseeable future.

Next, she went to the rack of pants, holding each pair up to him until she'd found a few in his size, or thereabouts. Then she pushed him into a change room with all the pants in his size, and held her breath.

She didn't have to wait long.

"Miss…Catena?"

"Mmm?"

"I seem to have a problem. These pants only have one button on the placket and I cannot seem to fasten them properly. Would you be kind enough to help me?"

"Sure," she said, ducking behind the curtain.

He'd picked a pair of skinny jeans, which hugged his butt to perfection, so they were definitely the right size, but the zipper had evidently flummoxed him. Catena dropped to her knees to help, only to find herself with a face full of…

"We forgot underwear!"

She'd never raced out of a change room so fast before.

Now she knew his size, it was easy to grab a few pairs of boxer briefs off the shelf, and throw a pair into the change room for him to put on.

The second time, she managed to avert her eyes from the prominent but well-covered bulge as she carefully zipped up his pants for him.

Then she rose to her feet, stepped back and…wow. Shirtless with skinny jeans suited him like he'd been born for them. Broad shoulders and all those muscles, tapering down to his abs, and a perfectly sculpted whatever it was you called that dip of his hips where the jeans hung. Denim caressed his well-muscled thighs, all the way down to his enormous bare feet. Like he'd just rolled out of bed and put them on…

Her mouth was dry as stone. Were all gargoyles this sexy, or was Tor just…special? All kinds of special… She wanted to jump into his lap and rub herself up against that bulge until…

"Miss Kelly, are you all right? You appear to be blushing."

Okay, it felt more like her cheeks were on fire, but if he'd been a picture on a calendar, she'd have licked it for sure.

"Maybe try some of the other pants on?" she suggested. "I'll…see if there's anything else that might fit you."

She waited long enough to make sure he knew how to unzip his jeans by himself before she beat a hasty retreat to the rack of shirts she'd dismissed earlier.

That's where she found it. A warm, dark winter coat, long enough to hide his wings and with enough space around the shoulders to fit comfortably, even with those wings. Wearing that, he might even be able to walk down the street past the Shut Up Café without anyone recognising him as the Moth Man.

When he stepped out of the change room to show her what had to be the most hideous pair of pants known to man – they looked like half of a white tuxedo that'd been rolled in newsprint – she wordlessly handed the coat over.

"Do men really wear pants like this?" he asked, staring down at the things.

"Well, given there's a whole lot of them here on the sale rack, I'm going to go with no on that one. Maybe try something else you do like?"

He nodded and headed back behind the curtain.

A long moment later, he emerged. He'd

picked wool suit pants that matched the coat…and made the jeans look like a mistake. These pants looked like they'd been made for him, perfectly tailored to accentuate the lines of his body, and with the coat thrown over the top, hanging open to reveal a hint of abs, he could have been a mafia boss, about to order her to do something outrageous. Just one look at him like this, and she knew she'd do it, too.

Then he lifted his head and his eyes met hers. There was something vulnerable in them, that didn't belong on such a powerful looking man. "I feel naked without a shirt and waistcoat," he admitted. "Even if this is the finest coat I've ever worn, it doesn't seem enough."

Together, they picked out a few shirts, the biggest ones Tayla had. If worst came to worst, they could always cut holes in the back for his wings, as long as he wore the coat over the top.

Tayla didn't stock many shoes, but the ones she did have met with Tor's approval, and they fitted, so Catena couldn't complain.

And when she saw Tor in his coat, with matching pants, shirt and shoes, her breath caught in her throat. His naked self already haunted her dreams, but this…this…he was every billionaire boss she'd ever lusted after in a book. Only better.

"Do I pass inspection?" Tor asked.

Catena grinned. It would probably cost her a week's wages, and she'd have to go without wine for a month, but seeing how sexy he looked made it worth every cent. "With flying colours," she said softly.

She led the way upstairs to her apartment. If she glanced behind her a few times to reassure herself that Tor really looked as good as she'd thought and he was coming home with her, well, that was only to be expected. The man was sex on a stick, naked or clothed.

Between the wings, the jeans and the suit, Tor could pass for pretty much every romance hero she'd ever read about. All in one incredible package. And yet, when he looked at her like he had in the change room, she sensed there was so much more to him than any character. Hidden depths she doubted even he truly knew about, what with his lack of memories about his past and all.

She could help him with that, for that was her calling. The true heart of an archaeologist — unearthing the secrets of the past and bringing them to light in the present.

The only question was: which did she want to uncover more, the sexy man or his secrets? She wasn't sure, but she suspected it might be both.

Which didn't bode well for her dreams tonight.

TWENTY-FIVE

"Oh, I'm starving. I know you don't eat, but did you want me to warm you up a bowl of pasta, so you can sit and sniff it while I have dinner?" Catena asked.

Sitting so close to her wouldn't be wise. Not when he could smell her scent as well as the food. Tor had grown uncomfortably hot in his fine new clothes, and even the memory of her touch as she'd helped him dress was making him hotter still.

He needed to get away from her, to cool off. "Thank you, but no. I think I'll go up on the roof instead."

Catena glanced out the window. "Are you sure? It's raining. You'll get soaked."

"Gargoyles don't mind the rain." And it would give him an excuse to take these pants off, which were growing tighter and tighter around his groin, the longer he stayed near her.

He dived into the wall, shimmying up through the walls until he reached the roof. He left his clothes on a beam in the ceiling cavity, where they'd stay dry, and ventured out into the open air.

A strong breeze gusted across the rooftop again, bringing with it a fine mist of rain and the slightest hint of salt, carried from the sea. Tor breathed deep, throwing his arms wide to embrace the chill. If he'd stayed in the same room as Catena for even a moment longer, he didn't know what he would have done. The ghost of her touch on his skin set his blood boiling in his veins…if he had blood, or veins. He did not know. What he did have were wings, which he flapped experimentally, catching the breeze just enough to lift him off his feet, before he drifted back down to the rooftop.

Did that mean he could fly? Of course, he had no memory of ever doing so, but he'd watched enough birds. If he merely flapped hard enough…

He soon found there was more to flight than just flapping. The angle of his body and his wings, that blasted breeze, and once he got himself aloft, there was the problem of landing, without falling flat on his face.

It might have been minutes or hours, but finally he managed to fly the length of the roof, then turn around and land on his feet. Triumph surged through him. He'd done it!

But it was one thing to skim along a rooftop, and another thing entirely to soar like the sea eagles that nested on a hill overlooking the harbour.

Nevertheless, he persisted.

Once he managed to get up high enough, the pesky breeze became his friend, buoying up his wings so that he could sail along almost effortlessly. It carried him inland, toward a walled compound atop the next hill.

Prison.

He knew it in his bones, no need to look for signs saying what the place was. It was a place of pain and loneliness. Sounds of the past still echoed in his memories, chilling him more completely than any rain shower. Clinking chains, the whistle and crack of a whip, the scrape of stone as it was pried from the hillside and turned into a terrible place where men were locked away.

No, he would not go there tonight. He had escaped and while he wasn't yet free, one day he would be, if he protected Catena.

Never mind the lustful feelings he'd had for her. He was in control of his body, and he would not give in to them. He was her protector, and he would protect her from every danger, until he was set free.

A note of rightness sounded in his head as this thought settled, though he could not explain how he knew what he did, or even how he'd be set free. Only that it would happen, if he was true to his purpose.

He returned to her house then, landing on the roof, before slipping back between the walls to work on repairing them again. There were some alarming leaks that let in rain, which might not be noticeable now, but would do a great deal of damage later, if they were not repaired immediately.

So he tucked his wings away, and set to work. Inside the house, Catena slept, safe and secure, and he intended to see that she stayed that way.

TWENTY-SIX

"Is that food? It smells like it might be, but I've never seen anyone eat something like that before," Tor said, leaning over the bench to peer at her plate.

Catena grinned. "This, my gargoyle friend, is a taco. Meat and beans and sauce and salad and salsa, with a heap of cheese, all crammed into a crispy corn shell. Messy as all hell to eat, but so worth it. I'd offer you one, so you could experience it for yourself, but…"

Tor forgot about the tacos and headed for the stove, where she'd left the pot of chili con carne. He stuck his head almost in the pot and inhaled. "I do not recognise the spices in this dish."

"I don't imagine chili was a big thing in Scotland, when you lived there. Or even here, when you arrived. The garlic's pretty much universal, though, I think." She frowned. "I'm not used to having a houseguest I can't cook for. Food is one of those things that brings people together, shared hospitality, that sort of thing. I can't even get you a drink, can I?"

Tor shook his head.

"So, of all your new clothes, you prefer Maria's old cargo pants, huh?" she asked.

Tor glanced down. "They are practical, sturdy, and have a great many pockets. Suitable attire for doing repairs about the house."

She swallowed her first bite of taco. Maybe she'd put in a bit too much chili this time. "So that's what you've been doing. I wondered why you weren't in the lounge room, watching movies."

"This is an old house, made with substandard materials. The limestone has cracked in places, and the plaster, too. Or maybe it is simply poor workmanship. Whatever the reason, it will not do. I have repaired what I could, replaced what I could not, and my next task is to patch all the leaks in the roof. Some are only tiny, but once moisture gets in, it tends to spread, and can ruin even the best-built house."

Catena drained her water glass, then refilled it. Definitely too much chili. "Wow. I didn't know your duties as my protector included home maintenance, too. You're amazing, Tor. A true treasure. I really should be paying you for this."

He waved her offer away, as if it was nothing. "I am merely fulfilling my purpose. The fine clothes you purchased yesterday cost more than I could earn in a lifetime. It seems only fitting that I repay you with service."

A lifetime of servitude for a couple of pairs of pants, a coat and some accessories? No. That was wrong on so many levels.

"Look, Tor, I don't know how much you might have earned in the past, but in case you haven't noticed, times have changed. A good bodyguard, or protector, earns more than I do on a librarian's pay, and tradesmen who do home maintenance earn even more than that, plus materials. I have no problem paying for a few clothes for you, especially when Tayla only charged me half price for them. Now you've patched up a few cracks, and helped me out when I needed it, we're more than even. You don't owe me anything."

Tor frowned. "But I am your protector, bound to serve you."

Catena threw her hands in the air. "Not by me! Who bound you, Tor? Because I think, instead of protecting me, you should be hunting the bastard down and making him set you free. You deserve to be free."

Tor nodded. "I will be free. But first I must

fulfil my purpose, and protect you." His frown deepened. "Do you not wish for me to protect you?"

Catena sighed. "You're a wish come true, Tor, in more ways than I can count. I wish you'd stay forever, but that's just me being selfish."

"It is not selfish at all, for I, too, wish to stay and protect you. Therefore, I shall stay."

"Tor…"

"Will you show me how to make the movies show on the screen?"

She sighed. Trying to explain the evils of slavery was lost on Tor. Maybe a movie would help. Or a TV show…

Oh, she had just the right one. "Sure," she said.

TWENTY-SEVEN

"My godmother, Maria, and I used to watch these all the time. I had a thing for the hunky archaeologist, Daniel Jackson, of course, but she preferred Teal'c or O'Neill. She always said she'd never met an archaeologist who loved his wife more than his work, but a warrior, a soldier, who protected his family and his friends, now he was the sort of person she would have wanted. She'd go all misty-eyed when she said that sometimes, like there had been someone like that, but it hadn't worked out, so she never married. I always wondered, but that's the one story she's never told me." Catena shook her head. "So, what did you think of *Stargate*?"

Tor squinted at the DVD cover in his hands, then back at the menu screen on the TV. "I do not understand how it is possible for people to travel to other planets, and for there to be people living on those planets."

Of course he'd missed the abolition of slavery storyline and gone straight to the heart of the show.

"They travel through a star gate, a sort of passage through space-time that connects two points on different planets." She'd heard the characters describe it enough. As long as Tor didn't expect her to explain or even understand wormhole physics…

"Does such a device truly exist?" he demanded.

"Well, no, not that we know of."

"Then it is not possible to travel to other planets, or for anyone to live there."

"Actually, I'm pretty sure they're planning the first manned mission to Mars, and possibly even a colony there. Maybe we should watch *The Martian*."

"Preposterous! Men living on Mars! The next thing you'll tell me is that there are men on the moon! I may not know everything about your time, Miss Kelly, but I am not a fool!"

Catena burst out laughing. "The moon landing was more than fifty years ago. I'm sure I can find you a movie or a documentary on that. Men have walked on the moon, and there are tardigrades there, too. And there is life on Mars. Just…not human life. Yet. I wish you could tell me how long you've slept, so I'd know how much history you've missed. Whoever did this to you deserves a big, fat, prickly cactus up the arse."

"What is a cactus?"

What else could she say, except: "A plant

you don't want anywhere near your arse!"

TWENTY-EIGHT

Persistent beeping echoed down the stairs. "That'll be the dryer," Catena said, getting up. "Do you want to pick something to watch next, while I go make the bed with the clean linen?"

Tor nodded, and she trudged upstairs to the laundry to silence the beeping.

When she returned, she had a frown on her face. "I've been terribly rude. All this time you've been here, and I should have offered you one of the guest rooms to sleep in. I can make one up with fresh linen in a few minutes, if you like. I shudder to think where you've been sleeping."

"Gargoyles never truly sleep," he assured her. "So I thank you for the kind offer, but I have no need for a bed."

She perched on the edge of the couch beside him. "What, not at all? You don't sleep? What about dreams? Do you have those?"

"In the darkness, before you called me, I was in a sort of wakeful doze. Not awake, but not asleep, either, because I was waiting for the call to arms. Afterwards…no, I haven't slept at all. I definitely haven't dreamed. There have been brief…I suppose you would call them flashes of memory, from before, but they're nothing like what you'd call a dream. Just memories of sights and sensations, there one moment and gone the next. Not like a dream, where you actually feel like you're there."

Her eyes lit up. "What do you remember?"

Tor winced. "The bad things, mostly. Moments of pain, or where I wish I'd done things differently. I fear my past was not a fit subject for a lady's ears, even a lady scholar like yourself."

Her eyes glistened with tears. "Sometimes memories hurt so much, it's almost impossible to talk about them. I can't imagine what you must have been through. But if you ever wish to unburden yourself, to talk about it, I'm pretty sure my lady's ears can handle it, and I'd be willing to listen. And if you ever find the man responsible for it, I will happily help you kick his arse. Or at least throw chili powder in his eyes."

Then she threw herself at him, in what he belatedly realised was a hug. The sweet smell of her hair overwhelmed him as she pressed her face into his chest. He didn't know if he had a heart any more, but something in there swelled at her touch. It took him a moment to get his arms around her to return the hug, then to pat her awkwardly on the back, before she released him and rose to her feet again, sniffling.

"So, if you don't sleep and you don't dream, what do you do at night?" she asked. She laughed a little. "Tell me you don't watch over me while I sleep. I mean, it sounds like a sweet, protective sort of thing to do, but it's still kind of creepy."

This was firmer ground, much less emotionally fraught.

"I work on your house, mostly, and I keep an eye on the house, knowing you're secure inside. And last night, I flew." This came out with considerable pride. He figured he was entitled to it, given how much work it had taken to manage his first flight.

"Holy hell, you can fly?" Her eyes lit up. "Will you take me with you?"

He couldn't refuse her, though he needed more practice before he'd dare to fly with her. As it was, he still wasn't sure he wouldn't fall out of the sky, and he'd never risk her life on his uncertain skills.

"When the rain clears up, and we have a fine night, I'd be honoured to fly with you. Perhaps on the night of the next new moon?" he said.

Catena beamed. "It's a date."

Tor had never been happier about not needing to sleep, for he'd need every spare moment to perfect his flying skills between now and then.

He would not let her fall.

TWENTY-NINE

"Are you ready, Miss Kelly?"

No. This was crazy. She was standing on her roof, about to fly around Fremantle with a freaking gargoyle, held up only by the power of his wings. If she fell to her death, she'd deserve it, doing something so stupid.

"Put your arms around my neck."

His arms tightened around her waist, warm and secure. He wasn't going to let go.

"Am I holding you too tight?" she asked breathlessly.

"I'm made of stone. No matter how tight your hold, you can't choke me, for I don't need to breathe. Now, hold on tight, for up we go!"

His wings spread wide, beating the air once, twice, three times, before her feet left the roof.

"A little higher, and we can catch an updraft. The wind will do the work for us." One beat. Another. "Ready? Here we go!"

Catena tried to look at the view as they soared upward, but the rush of wind from his wings stung, forcing her to close her eyes.

As if he could feel her discomfort, Tor said, "Don't worry, you're safe in my arms. I won't let you go until we're safe on the ground again."

Shit. Him landing in the middle of High Street, with her in his arms, in front of a café full of people with camera phones…Catena's stomach swooped, threatening to bring her dinner back up again. She swallowed. "On the roof. We'll be landing on the roof."

"Wherever you wish, when you wish. Now, if you want to stop."

He tilted and turned, and suddenly the wind wasn't in her face any more. Maybe it hadn't been his wings to blame at all, but the weather trying to spoil their flight.

"No, I've always liked flying," she said.

She felt him stiffen in surprise. "You've flown before?"

Catena laughed. "Of course. In a plane. I'm sure you've seen them – flashing lights, on their wingtips, high up in the sky? Higher than you can fly?"

"Another mystery I had meant to ask you about. Thank you." His wings flapped, but they seemed to have stopped moving. "Where would you like to go?"

She took a deep breath. "Wherever you'd like to take me. Show me…a view you wish to share."

THIRTY

Tor hadn't expected that. He thought for a moment. The best thing about being able to fly was the view from up here, higher than anyone else, and the freedom to land wherever he wanted, or fly away again, as the fancy took him.

What he wanted was to hold Catena in his arms forever, breathing in her scent as she pressed her soft body against him. But he didn't want to fly too high or too far with her, lest he tire his wings to much and he'd have to make her walk home. That would be an ignominious end he didn't even want to contemplate. He might not be able to fly forever with her in his arms, but he wanted to do it again, and again and again, something she'd never allow if he messed this up.

So he surveyed the port city, spread out before him, and picked a tall building that towered over all the others, but had a flat roof that would be forgiving if he botched the landing. Fremantle Hospital, the sign out the front said, in big, red letters.

He glided in, then tipped his wings back and dropped, bending his knees to soften the landing as he hit the roof. You could see the whole city from here – the fishing boat harbour, the twinkling lights of the city buildings, and the well-lit port at the river mouth beyond.

"What's that?" Catena asked.

Instead of looking at the view, she was

pointing at a two storey building behind the hospital.

Tor blinked. A building he knew.

"That's the Knowle, the Comptroller General's residence. Built for a man named Henderson, who was in charge of all the convicts here," he said.

Memories stirred, of paper plans crackling in his hands. Architectural plans, of a beautiful house that was smaller than the building it had now become, but still a great house.

"How do you know that?" she asked. "I've lived here all my life, and I didn't even know it existed."

"Because I built it," he said. That had been in the early days here, when they still respected him, saw him as the master mason he was, and not some common convict. He'd turned their crude shell of a commissariat into a proper warehouse, where goods could be stored without the waves carrying them away every time there was a storm, so they'd been only too happy to hand over the construction of the grand house to him. A house that stood still.

"You…built it…" she said slowly. "You remember?"

"A little," he admitted. Common labourers had cut the stone, and he'd directed them where he wanted it, fitting them seamlessly together into walls to stand the test of time. Those had been good days. Then the engineers had arrived, and they'd started building the prison…

"What was Fremantle like then? I can't even imagine…" she breathed, then shivered.

There might not be a breeze, but clear nights could get cold, as well he knew. Tor wrapped his wing around her, pulling her to his side, to keep her warm.

He stretched out his hand to point. "Most of the buildings here weren't even built yet, and the port was out there, not in the river. Tall ships bobbing at anchor, a forest of masts as far as the eye could see. Bringing supplies and convicts, for the colony had little more than timber and stone of its own, even then.

None of this grassed Esplanade, either. Just a stretch of shore, which flooded at every high tide. The waves would wash up the steps of the buildings along the shore, and sometimes even inside. They were all warehouses then, even the Esplanade Hotel. Places to store goods and men in chains, identified by numbers, not names. Every second building was a hotel or a drinking house. There was even a whole street of brothels..." He remembered himself. "Beg pardon, Miss Kelly. I should not have spoken of those."

She laughed. "Have you ever been in one, Tor? Handed over hard-earned cash for a night of wanton sex? Or could you only afford an hour? I've heard stories about the brothels back in the gold rush days. They had the girls in stalls like a horse stable, and they spent the whole night on their feet, up against the stall wall."

If it were possible, Tor would be blushing furiously. "It seems you know more than I do, Miss Kelly. I have never...I mean, I did not…"

"You've never paid for sex, I take it. Or worked in a brothel. Well, that makes two of us. I'm not sure I could share my body with a stranger like that. To be that close to someone I didn't love, or at least have feelings for…" She gave a shudder, which set every nerve in his wing afire. No, his whole body.

She was close to him. Did that mean she had fond feelings for him? He didn't dare hope, and yet…

"What else was built then? I know the Round House was…"

Tor mentally shook himself, and tried to remember. The memories came easier now. Maybe it was because of her, because she'd asked him. He was hers to command, after all.

"The Round House was there, yes, and the commissariat, the building that is the Shipwreck Gallery now, with all the anchors out the front. The warders' cottages, all those houses along there. The prison was still being built, the southern half of the building there now, along with the walls and the gatehouse. They hollowed out the hill for it, quarrying the stone, then lifting it to the top of what remained of the hill, to make it harder for the prisoners to escape. Of course, that only made the wall unstable..." He trailed off. Pointing out the wall's weaknesses had earned him chains and pain. He was surprised to see the wall still standing. He opened his mouth to comment on it.

"I can't imagine what the convicts thought about all of it. I mean, I know they were criminals, convicted of some rather horrible crimes, which they deserved to pay for, a debt to society, and they did, building this city and High Street and so many other things, but to make them build their own prison. I mean, even the most hardened criminal had to have broken at the thought of those tiny cells, those thick walls, to know that when it was finished, there'd be no escape..."

Yes. That's why he'd listened to the butcher, and taken his chance before the walls were finished. Trading one form of servitude for another, but his choice had brought him her. She was in his arms now, and even if he was only her protector, it was more than he could have ever hoped before, when his whole future looked to be locked up in a limestone cell…

"I guess they got what they deserved," she said softly.

They did, but not him. He wanted what he didn't deserve. That's what had gotten him into this mess in the first place, a man daring to look above his station. He wouldn't make the same mistake again.

"I imagine they did," he said, for he was no longer one of them when the prison opened, and they were locked away.

"Tor?"

He stared at her. How long had he been lost in thought, completely ignoring her?

"It's really lovely up here, and I'm grateful you took me for a flight, but I'm absolutely freezing right now, even with your wing around me, and I'm afraid if I don't get home and warm soon, I won't be able to feel my feet."

Some protector he was.

"Of course. If you'd put your arms around my neck again?"

This time, he scooped her up in his arms, cuddling her to his chest to keep her warm, as he flew her home.

THIRTY-ONE

He touched down on the roof with only the slightest bump, and the flight was over. Catena cursed herself for not wearing warmer clothing. She could have flown with him forever, or at least until his wings gave out.

Tor set her on her feet, his wings curving around to shelter her from the cold night air, just like he had on the hospital roof. She hadn't expected them to be so soft, like well-oiled leather, though he'd assured her they were living stone, just like the rest of him. Whatever that meant.

She looked up, meeting his eyes, and found herself lost in them. She swallowed. "Thank you, Tor, for taking me up there with you, and sharing some of your memories. If you ever want to do that again, I would…I would…"

Now who was forgetting things? Words. She had no words. Just his eyes, lost in his eyes, as warm wings wrapped around her, pulled her against him. Strong hands cupped her cheeks as he bent his head…

His kiss exploded against her lips, setting her whole body alight. She'd read about tongues dancing, but this was…this was…no words. She didn't know where her mouth ended and his began, and she didn't care. If this was how gargoyles kissed, then she never wanted to kiss a man again.

And then…she stood alone, separated from him by a metre of icy air, and a world of difference she did not understand. Her tongue tasted like dust and chalk.

I licked him and now he's mine. The thought surfaced, then sank like the stone it was. Dead stone.

Because he wasn't hers, no matter how much she wished he could be. Between the flight and that supernatural kiss, and everything he'd done for her, not to mention a body that could have…no, had…featured in her wildest fantasies, Tor was everything she could possibly want in a man. The sort of man who made a girl think of forever…

But that was just it, wasn't it? Tor wasn't a man. He was a gargoyle, a creature of myth and legend, one she couldn't even begin to understand. He was only here because he believed he should be her protector, and it was only a matter of time before he realised there was nothing holding him here, that she didn't need a protector, no matter how much she wanted him. He'd already lived for two centuries, and he'd live for who knew how many more, while she'd be lucky to get one, and if this was all the time she'd get with him, then it was more than she had any right to expect.

He was a dream, and she was just a part-time librarian, who dreamed of doing a PhD, but hadn't even managed to pick a project, while he'd built mansions that had stood for centuries. Every moment he gave her was a precious gift.

"Thank you," she whispered, then ran into the house.

THIRTY-TWO

Madness overcame him. That's what it must have been, he told himself later.

But the moment her feet touched that rooftop, she'd shivered, and his wings had closed around her automatically. Protecting her from the very air itself, if that was what she needed.

She raised her head, her eyes filled with yearning. With need. Kiss me, they'd seemed to say, and he was powerless to resist her unspoken command.

His wings cocooned her, pulling her close even as they hid her from the world, so that she was his alone, if only for this moment. Her soft, warm body, shivering slightly against his sensitive wing membranes. Until he found himself shivering, too, in anticipation.

He dared to raise his hands to her face, and, miracle of miracles, her eyes radiated approval, urging him on. Never had he felt skin so soft, pure delight beneath his rough workman's hands.

She parted her lips, drew in a sharp little breath, and her eyes begged him to kiss her.

And he was hers, bound to obey her in all things.

The moment his lips touched hers, a flood of sensation rushed through him. His heart raced within his chest, blood pumping through his veins so powerfully it felt like he was fizzing inside. Her tongue twined with his, and he swore he could taste her, a heady mix of spices and salt. Lightheaded, he kissed her like she was air itself, and he once more needed to breathe.

Blood pooled in his groin, anticipating what might come after this kiss. For Catena had her hands on his chest, but they were drifting lower, and when she reached the waistband of his pants, her hands would dip lower, she'd take hold of him with both hands, and...

No. He was her protector, and he must protect her. Even against himself. She was a lady, and he was her servant, a lowly escaped convict who did not deserve even this stolen kiss.

He wrenched himself away, letting the night air drink the heat between them, until he was cold stone once more. Her protector. No more, no less.

Tears of pity filled her eyes, maybe for him, maybe mourning the unholy connection they had shared for one precious moment. Never again. She knew, better than he did, that this could not be.

She turned and dashed back into the house.

Every particle in his body yearned to follow her, to claim a second kiss, but Tor was master here, not his body, and he knew his body yearned for things it could never have.

Instead, he resolved to treasure the memory of that one precious kiss, and the moment he'd almost felt like a man again, instead of a monster made of stone.

THIRTY-THREE

When a storm front came through, it was almost a relief. Wind blew the rain in sideways, revealing a whole new raft of leaks for Tor to repair, allowing him to avoid Catena easily. He worked furiously to finish, because another army of storm clouds were already massing in the west, bringing the sort of winter storm he could have sworn followed him all the way from Scotland.

He'd managed to wedge himself into a particularly tricky corner, where the maze of wooden beams meeting made it almost impossible to reach the leak, unless he contorted himself as sinuously as a snake. Even then…

A scream rang out, curiously amplified by the shape of the ceiling cavity, as though Catena was in danger directly beneath him. He shot through the ceiling, but found the bathroom empty. Tor raced from room to room, calling her name.

He found her in the lounge, clutching a cup in white-knuckled hands, her eyes wide with fear.

"What is it? What's happened?" he demanded, scanning the room.

"I don't know. Someone screamed. It must be Anemone next door."

"I'll go," he began, striding toward the nearest wall.

Catena held up her hand. "No. She's a widow and she lives alone. If you burst in on her the way you did with me, you'll give her a heart attack. I'll go, and you can…watch my back, from the wall behind me, or something. If I need you, I'll call, and you can appear like a normal person, and not alarm her."

"But if anything happens to you…"

"You'll be right there, ready to help me deal with it. Right?"

He was not imagining the fiery determination in her eyes. This was a command he could not refuse, no matter how much it pained him.

"Right," he said reluctantly.

She rose. " Let's go."

She marched out the front door, and across the landing to the door to the other apartment. Tor stood at her side, every step of the way, hidden in the wall beside her. He had only to reach out his fingers, and he'd be able to grip her shoulder.

Not that he intended to touch her again. After that unforgivable kiss, he didn't dare.

Catena rapped smartly on the door.

"Anemone? It's Catena from next door. Are you all right?"

A muffled voice came from the other side of the door, followed by approaching footsteps. Approaching fast. The door was flung open, and a tiny, breathless woman with short, curled hair covered in plaster dust stood there. "Um, hi?"

Something dark moved in the crook of the woman's arm, before two pointy ears popped up, also dusted with white. The cat sneezed twice, then squirmed out of the woman's grip and dropped to the floor.

"I heard you scream, and I just came to check to see if you were all right," Catena said.

Anemone blinked. "Oh, fine, fine. Now, anyway. Some of the rain got into the roof, and part of the ceiling in my bathroom collapsed. Water and wiring everywhere. It's all right now, though. I've turned the power off at the fuse box. I'll call an electrician in the morning. After I've had a chance to clean up the mess."

The tiny black cat marched up to the wall, right where Tor was, and began rubbing her head against his leg, as if the beast knew he was there. Then she began to purr.

"Sorry, she's been scent marking the walls a lot lately. I have no idea what's gotten into her," Anemone said, reaching for the cat.

Puss dodged between both Catena and Anemone's legs, then made a dash back inside Anemone's house.

"Well, let me know if you need any help with anything. I'm just across the hall," Catena said, turning to head home.

Anemone started to close her door. Through the gap, Tor glimpsed the cat, staring intently at him, until the door clicked shut.

THIRTY-FOUR

Catena was debating whether she had the patience to make pancakes for breakfast, or if she should stick with cereal, when she heard a knock at her front door.

Surprised, she opened it, to find Anemone standing there, looking much more herself. Her short curls were back to pale gold, instead of dusted white, so she looked more like her own age than a little old lady. The cat was nowhere to be seen.

"I'm sorry to bother you so early," Anemone began.

Catena shrugged. "I've been up for a while. I was about to make my second cup of coffee."

"Oh, no worries, then. Well, actually, maybe. This is going to sound really strange…"

Catena pressed her lips together so she wouldn't laugh. Nothing Anemone could say would be stranger than discovering she had a gargoyle houseguest.

"Okay, I thought it was really weird, but…while I was cleaning up the mess from last night, I found a shoe. A kid's shoe."

Catena knew Anemone was a widow, but she couldn't be much older than thirty. If she'd had kids, Catena would have heard them by now.

"Look, it's…it reminded me of some of the ones in the museum collection. Really old and solid. It looked like it had been in the roof for a while." Anemone sighed. "I'm not saying this very well, am I? I work in conservation. I don't find things, other people find them, and then they bring them to me to make sure they're preserved. Or find out if they can be preserved. Archaeology's more your area, and I remember you saying you knew the family who used to live in my apartment before I bought it... Look, you said last night to ask you if I needed help with anything. I don't really need it, it's just...there was a child's shoe hidden in my house. If you'd found it, wouldn't you want to know more? Maybe even find out who its owner was?"

Breakfast was overrated, anyway. "Yeah, I'd totally want to solve the shoe mystery, if it was me. Give me a minute to grab my camera and some brushes and I'll be right over. I can't promise I'll be able to find anything more than we know already, but I can at least take a look and do things properly, so we have something to go on if you want to dig a bit deeper."

Fifteen minutes later, armed with a camera, a brush kit and a coverall, Catena stepped into

Anemone's apartment.

"I stopped sweeping up the moment I found the shoe, so you could see it in situ as much as possible," Anemone said.

Catena nodded. Anemone might not be an archaeologist herself, but she'd evidently worked with enough of them to know their process.

She tried not to stare as she followed Anemone through the house. Her place had plenty of space and she'd happily live there for as long as Maria would let her, but it was obvious when the house had been split into two apartments, Anemone's was the grander one. Even the bathroom, with its enormous claw foot tub, was more decadent than Catena's.

Of course, Catena's modest bathroom wasn't covered with plaster dust, with a big, gaping hole where the ceiling should be, so there was that.

She set down her ruler beside the small shoe, taking pictures from several angles before brushing through the debris around it.

"I'm sorry, I found it while I was sweeping, so I picked it up. By the time I'd realised…I'd already brushed some of the dust off it, and it was already on its side, so most of the crap inside it had fallen out," Anemone said.

Catena shrugged. "It's not like it's Tutankhamen's tomb, the sort of treasure the whole world will want to know about." She pointed up at the ceiling. "Is there any chance I could have a look up there?"

"Sure. I'll go get the stepladder."

When she returned, Catena had to climb up carefully, because there was a web of electrical cables tangled together across the gap.

"They're turned off at the main switchboard, I promise. If they were live, they'd still be sparking. They're safe," Anemone said, as if reading Catena's mind.

She considered waiting until dark, when she'd know Tor would be around, watching out for her in true protector fashion, but he'd said he hid in the walls during the day, so maybe he was already here. Just hidden. Bolstered by that thought, she kept going to the top of the ladder, until she was well into the roof cavity.

Well, she could see where the water had come from – a little rivulet ran down from a gap in the stones, where the roof met the wall. She silently thanked Tor for fixing up her side of the building, or her ceiling might be lying in pieces on the floor, just like Anemone's.

Lifting her camera, she snapped a picture of the rafters and beams, caked in dust and what looked like rat droppings. Ugh. Wait, was that…?

She zoomed in and took a couple of pictures first, before she dared disturb it.

"Hey, Anemone, could you pass up my brushes and that ruler? I think I might have found another one." Up came the roll of brushes, with the ruler stuck in the middle. Catena thanked her, then said, "Could you hold the ladder steady? I'll need to stretch a bit…"

She edged the ruler onto the beam beside the shoe, and took some more pictures. Then she reached for the ruler again, and somehow it snagged on the shoe and sent it tumbling down into the bathroom below.

Catena swore, then had to hold tight to the ladder as it wobbled, while Anemone dodged the shower of debris the shoe brought down with it.

Nope. Catena had had enough. She climbed down again, coughing all the way.

As she reached the floor, something moved in the corner of her eye, on the wall. Was that a…?

She blinked, and it was gone, but she could have sworn she'd seen a penis sticking out of the wall. Tor was definitely here. What had he done with his pants?

The little cat Anemone had been carrying yesterday sidled into the room and rubbed her head against the wall where the penis had appeared. As if she knew Tor was in there, too.

They were going to have words when she

got home. Pointing his penis at her neighbours…

Anemone nudged the new shoe with her foot. "It looks like a pair."

Shoes. Yes. That was a much safer topic.

Catena knelt down and brushed the dirt away from the new shoe. Anemone was right. The shoes looked like they were made of leather, hard and cracked from too many hot summers in the roof. But what on earth were they doing there?

She knew kids stashed stuff and forgot about it, but this kid couldn't have been more than a toddler, and there was no way a toddler could've crawled up into the roof to put them there. It made no sense.

She tucked her brushes back into their bag, and rolled it up. "Well, I've got some pictures, and I'll do a bit of research with those. What do you want to do with the shoes?"

Anemone shrugged. "I don't know. I guess I'll do what we always do in the museum when something new comes in. Bag 'em and freeze them to kill any bugs."

"Sounds like a plan. Well, I'd best go have some breakfast, and I'll let you know what I find. And if you do need any help with any thing – repairs, whatever, let me know, all right? Just because we live alone, doesn't mean we are alone." Catena glared at the wall.

Anemone glanced around nervously. "Yes. Well. Thank you. I should probably finish cleaning up in here so I can have a shower."

"Yeah, I'll need one, too, after that."

Catena headed home, her camera swinging with every step. She should be putting together her PhD project proposal, but it could wait a bit. She had a new mystery to solve, and she wouldn't be able to focus until she knew whose shoes they were.

THIRTY-FIVE

It being Sunday, the day of Catena's customary visit to her godmother, it only seemed fitting that she start her shoe research at the source: Maria, whose family had owned the building since the first stone was laid. She'd told her the story once, of the family matriarch, who'd come to the Swan River Colony on a sailing ship with her children, summoned by a husband who was nowhere to be found when she'd arrived. She became an established businesswoman in her own right, in order to provide for her children, and Maria was her last surviving descendant, so when she'd wanted to go into archaeology instead of getting married or getting a proper job, her parents hadn't been able to object, though they'd certainly grumbled. They'd died before Catena was born, so she'd never met them.

"She's having a good day today," one of the nurses told her outside Maria's room.

That could mean anything, so Catena didn't get her hopes up that Maria might recognise her today. She'd given up on that when Maria had entered the nursing home.

"Hi, Maria. I brought Tim Tams this week, a new flavour. Would you believe they made tiramisu ones?"

"The original ones are the best," Maria grumbled.

"Oh, that's not true! My favourite are the caramel ones, and occasionally the white chocolate ones, when they bring out a special edition for Christmas."

"My goddaughter liked the caramel ones. But you had to put them in the fridge overnight, so the caramel would get all hard and chewy, like toffee."

Maria smiled. Yes, Maria had never forgotten to chill them first.

The tea trolley appeared then, and the lady wheeling it wouldn't rest until she'd made both of them a cup of coffee, plus handed over a bunch of biscuits. Heaven help any of the residents who were diabetic, or maybe that's why Maria got so many – she was the only resident who wasn't.

Catena blew on her coffee to cool it. "I have a funny story to tell you today, about the neighbours in the apartment next door to yours."

Maria's face clouded, and Catena knew she had to capture her interest fast, or she'd ask the inevitable question of when she could go home, forcing Catena to say, "When you're better," which really meant never.

"There was a really bad storm the other night, wind blowing the rain in sideways. So water got into the roof, pooled at the lowest point, as it does, until the ceiling collapsed under its weight. Whoosh! An indoor storm of water and plaster."

Maria chuckled. "I bet that gave everyone a surprise."

"It did! The lady who lived there screamed so loud, she gave me a fright, and there was such a mess. The bathtub was full of plaster, and that's a big bathtub."

Maria grinned. "Big enough for two. That's why I bought it, though I never did get to christen it myself. Pity."

Catena was willing to bet a week's pay there was a story there, but she couldn't pursue it now – she had to ask about the shoes.

"So she had a huge job to clean it all up. And, right there in the middle of the mess, she found a pair of shoes!"

Catena pulled out her phone and flipped through the pictures until she found the right one. Both shoes, sitting beside a ruler on the floor.

"So tiny and made of thick leather. Maybe even as old as the house. Do you know who put them there?"

Maria took the phone and squinted at the picture. "Late Victorian, I'd say, or maybe a little later. In the ceiling, you say? What a strange place to put a pair of shoes!"

Catena's heart sank. "So you don't know who might have put them there? Maybe one of your ancestors, who lived there before you did?"

Maria shook her head. "Those apartments were offices when I inherited the building, and they were offices for as long as I can remember. I had them turned into apartments when my parents died. I was going to keep the big, grand one for myself, but I was travelling about so much back then, from one dig to another, that I didn't need all that space when it was just me, and only between digs…"

"So no one lived there at all?" Catena

persisted.

Maria considered. "Well, not that I know of. Maybe when it was built, the owners lived upstairs for a bit. A lot of businesses did that back then, with the shop downstairs and the house upstairs, until they could afford something bigger and better. You're lucky it was only shoes. Some of the digs I've worked on – houses that were abandoned long ago, so you'd think there'd be nothing left, but the things they buried under the floors! There was this one medieval village, wiped out by the plague, and every house had a cat skeleton under the hearth. Some of them even had plague-infected rats laid beside them – yes, they tested the rats, and found the plague bug, I forget its Latin name. Ugh, I stayed away from medieval digs after that – I mean, who wants to catch the plague?"

"No one," Catena said.

"But the cats weren't the worst thing, not by a long shot. Some of the other digs I've worked at had human bodies buried in the most unexpected places. Under the city gates, or under the threshold of each house. Sometimes even entombed in the walls." Maria shuddered. "Some of them looked to have been buried alive, left with some food and water. Some of them appeared to be slaves, or captured enemies, slaughtered as sacrifices to protect the building. The worst ones were the children. I know the infant mortality rate was high, but you never expect to find a baby's skeleton under the hearth of a house.

"There were lots of theories about them, of course. Only a small part of archaeology is digging, while the rest is coming up with theories to explain what you've found. Some said the babies had been illegitimate, or unwanted. Others said they'd died young and were buried where their angelic spirits would protect the house, sort of like Catholics believed the remains of kids killed at the time of Jesus's birth were somehow holy relics, and could protect churches. That's still a thing today, too – can't have a church without some pieces of a saint inside it. Strange superstition.

"Some academics said the slain enemies were supposed to protect the house, too. Seems perverse, if you ask me. Killing someone for attacking your home, then burying them at the front door so they could rise up and defend your home against the next set of invaders. As if having an army of zombie skeletons would be a good thing…imagine the smell! I can't imagine corpses would be particularly good protectors. But there's no accounting for religious beliefs, and human sacrifice has been a thing for pretty much as far back as we can tell. Doesn't matter the religion."

Catena felt slightly ill. She set her coffee cup down and pushed it away. "I wish I hadn't asked."

Maria reached over and patted her hand. "Digging them up wasn't so bad. It wasn't until afterward, when the forensic reports came back, that we found out how they'd died. Horribly, in most cases. No, if you want to know which bodies were the most disgusting to dig up, it was the ones who'd been mummified. All sorts of natural processes could mummify a body, and instead of a skeleton, suddenly you're face to face with a dead guy who still has a face..."

Maria always had been a fan of horror movies.

After several more stories about bog bodies and mummies, even Maria's enthusiasm began to wane. She wanted to be out in the field again, discovering things, not trapped in a hospital bed with incomplete memories. She'd complained about it to Catena often enough, and she could see her winding up for another rant.

"Sorry, love, visiting hours end in five minutes," a nurse said.

Catena shot to her feet, pushed the pack of remaining Tim Tams toward Maria, and said her goodbyes.

It wasn't until she reached the car park that she allowed her shoulders to slump in defeat.

Maria hadn't known anything about the shoes, or any previous residents, if indeed anyone had lived there.

She'd have to do things the hard way.

THIRTY-SIX

Spurred on by Maria's horror stories about foundation sacrifices, Catena switched on her laptop as soon as she got home. Normally, she'd go straight to the peer-reviewed journal databases to answer an archaeological mystery, but something made her choose to search the wider internet instead. After all, how many archaeological investigations took place in ceilings?

More than she'd expected, that was for sure. Maria's tales were just the tip of the iceberg.

Bodies buried in houses, tales of cats and…there were even global databases of found objects like Anemone's shoes. Databases managed by reputable institutions, not just crazy conspiracy theorists or other hobbyists.

The practice was witchcraft, pure and simple. Except hardly pure and far from simple.

And the pictures...she'd have to watch all the Alien movies to get these images out of her head.

Shoes and cats and people and gloves and the nauseating practice of witch bottles...it was all there, in graphic detail.

Putting shoes in a house was supposed to be a substitute for the shoes' owner, either to elicit protection for the shoes' owner, or protection from the shoes' former owner after their death. When the item belonged to a child, sometimes it was supposed to bring fertility, or reduce infant mortality within the household.

And if a child's shoes were hidden in the house…what else was there? This building had half a dozen fireplaces – there could be more than just a pair of shoes concealed within them. There could even be bodies…

God, what if there were bodies buried in her house?

But one theme ran through all of the articles, no matter who wrote them: protection.

The one thing Tor kept talking about. How it was his purpose.

What if his body was hidden somewhere within the walls? And the Tor she'd talked to, who walked through walls and flew through the air, was the result of a foundation sacrifice?

Catena switched off the laptop and buried her head in her hands.

THIRTY-SEVEN

Tor slotted the last sliver of stone into the mortar and smoothed it so it sat flush against the blocks on either side. There. The job was done. Catena's house would stand for a century more, if he was any judge, and he knew he was.

Unlike her neighbour, the house held no danger for her.

He really should tell her the good news.

He found her seated at a desk, behind a small screen not dissimilar to the one they watched their movies on. Instead of the device Catena had called a remote control, this screen had a board with different buttons on it flat on the desk before her, labelled with the letters of the alphabet. She occasionally touched these, but seemed to prefer waving her fingers in front of the screen. The screen, to his amazement, recognised the movements and the picture changed accordingly.

Damn, but she could read fast. The words travelled from the bottom of the page to the top as her finger directed them upward, her frown growing deeper with every line.

Then her mouth opened wide in horror, and she stabbed a finger at the screen. The words vanished, replaced by a picture of a cat. She stared at it for a long moment, shuddered, then sent it back into the aether, too.

The screen slowly faded to black, but she still stared at it, as though she could see something he could not. Perhaps. Scholars saw things far more deeply than a simple stonemason like him. Stuff he couldn't even begin to understand.

Still, he did understand that whatever she had seen, it had made her far from happy, and he longed to cheer her up. Dare he step out of the wall and offer her a few words of comfort? He wouldn't kiss her again, but a word or two could not hurt.

"God, Tor, tell me you're not here. Stuck in the walls, or beneath the floor. I just can't bear the thought."

Not only did she not want his sympathy, she wanted him gone. His heart broke for her.

Silently, he stepped back and fled to the roof instead. Tor spread his wings and flew off into the night, heedless of the rain streaming down his face in a poor imitation of Catena's tears.

THIRTY-EIGHT

Catena barely slept that night, jerking awake a thousand times from nightmares of skeleton or zombie armies bursting out of the walls, but she had to work on Monday morning, so she dragged herself to the work kitchen for an extra coffee before the library opened.

Callie was in there with a glass teapot, brewing up something that smelled like it belonged in a perfume bottle, not a teacup.

"You been up late reading again? Was he hot?"

Catena just shook her head. She couldn't stop staring at the teapot. A witch's brew, that's what it looked like. Then her sluggish mind caught up with her eyes. "What do you know about foundation sacrifices, and hiding shoes in ceilings?"

Callie grinned. "Are you planning on taking up dark magic? I think I have some medieval spellbooks on those things. Not for the faint-hearted, though – there are some pretty stomach-churning ingredients in those. Even the spells that don't involve corpses."

"Could you…could you take a look for me, and let me know what you find out?" Catena asked.

"That medieval magic was pretty fucked up? I can tell you that right now. Anyone who thinks killing someone to strengthen their walls instead of just building a better fucking wall has some serious issues. Makes Shakespeare look like Disney."

Catena already knew that. "No, it's just that

my neighbour found a pair of baby shoes in her ceiling, and if someone who believes in that stuff put them there, there's no knowing what else might be hidden in the house. It's more than a hundred years old, and…Callie, what if the original builder was a serial killer, only no one knew because the bodies are in the walls?"

"Someone would have noticed people going missing."

"Not always."

Callie sighed, then poured herself a cup of tea. "All right, I'll take a look through some of my witchcraft texts and see what I can find. Anything else? As long as it's not the Moth Man, I have time for a bit of research in the inter semester break."

Catena hesitated. What harm could it do? "Gargoyles. Anything you can find about them."

"Okay. I've never heard of anyone having a gargoyle problem before. Rats, yes. Cockroaches, definitely. But gargoyles? I know they're ugly, but so's wallpaper, and people still buy that."

"Not all gargoyles are ugly," Catena blurted out, without thinking.

Callie considered for a moment. "Okay, maybe some of the Disney ones are kind of cute, and there was that musclebound one who was pretty hot for a cartoon, but I think the whole point of gargoyles is to scare away threats. Pretty won't work for that."

Catena made herself nod. Better than telling Callie the truth about Tor. She'd be carted off to the nuthouse before she could blink.

"Just checking…you want this info for research purposes only, because you're an archaeologist and you live in a historical site? You're not trying to summon something from the nether hells to protect your house from zombies, right? Because none of that stuff is possible. Trust me, I know. I have a library full of Latin texts with instructions on how to do those things, and not a single history text that actually says someone succeeded. I mean, witch burnings would've been a whole different beast if the witches had summoned demons to protect them, if you get my drift."

For the first time since she'd left Maria's nursing home, Catena managed a smile. "Nope. I'm all about banishing demons, not summoning them."

"Good. Now, tempus fugit…don't you have a library to open?"

Catena glanced at the clock. "Shit."

Callie's gentle laughter followed her all the way across the courtyard.

THIRTY-NINE

Anemone's lights were on when Catena got home, so instead of heading for her own front door, she crossed the landing and knocked on Anemone's.

She answered it with a glass of wine in her hand. "What can I do for you?"

"I thought you might like to know what I've found out about your shoes," Catena said.

"Oh! That was fast. Come in. We're just

finishing up dinner." Anemone opened the door wide, gesturing for Catena to enter.

Catena hung back. "I didn't know you had company. I can come back later, or another day, if you like."

Anemone blinked, then laughed softly. "Oh, no, it's just me and the cat. Come in and see."

Catena relented and followed her inside. In the kitchen, she found a near-empty bowl on the bench, beside a slow cooker that emitted the most amazing aroma.

"Oh, what is that?" she asked.

"A Hungarian style goulash. It takes about two days to cook, so I do a huge batch and freeze it in, or I'd be eating it for every meal for a week. Here, I'll get you some." Anemone pulled a clean bowl out of the cupboard and began spooning the stew into it. When it was brimming, she held it out to Catena. "It goes really well with a slice or two of heavy bread. I picked up that sourdough fresh from the bakery this morning."

"Oh, I couldn't…" Catena began.

"Sure you can. There's heaps. It's the least I can do, if you've found the owner of my mystery shoes."

"Yeah, that might not be as easy as I thought…"

Between bites – God it was good – Catena told Anemone what she'd found out so far.

Anemone just sat there nodding and sipping her wine.

When Catena was done, Anemone asked, "So you think a witch put them there?"

Catena almost choked.

"Let me get you some wine," Anemone said. "I used a whole bottle in the goulash, so I had to open a second bottle to drink."

Catena had to admit the shiraz suited the stew perfectly.

She cleared her throat. "I don't know about a witch, but it looks like the shoes were probably put there as part of some fertility or protection ritual. Whether they actually do anything is anyone's guess, and I suppose it depends on what you believe."

Anemone looked thoughtful. "So I should put them back, then?"

"If you believe in that sort of thing, I guess it can't hurt. If they weren't doing anything, then it shouldn't really matter."

"There are more things in heaven and Earth than are dreamt of in your philosophy," Anemone murmured. "From what you've said, it seems they're supposed to be hidden near the hearth, not up in the roof. I might put them back into one of the fireplaces instead, up the chimney. Seeing as they weren't doing any good where they were."

"Well, no…" Catena wasn't really sure what to say. She hadn't expected Anemone to be so superstitious, but then she hadn't expected gargoyles to exist, either, and she hadn't imagined Tor.

"Is there anything else I should do? You mentioned protective marks…"

When had Catena become an expert in arcane rituals? "Well, in the other buildings where shoes and things were found, there was always more than one, in different places. And marks carved or burned into walls and doorways and hearthstones. As if the people who believed in such things thought the more protection they had, the better, right?"

"Well, I know it was certainly the case with the prison. The main buildings are pretty much pristine, with very little graffiti on the walls except where the prisoners got permission to do artwork, in the last days before it was closed. There's not a single convict mark from construction on the main cell block, or the gatehouse. But the walls are a different story. Especially the north wall, which blew over in a storm the year after it was built."

Catena gaped. "A storm blew the limestone wall over? Seriously? Those walls have to be thicker than the walls of this place, and about as high. To think a gust of wind could just tip that over…wow. Just…wow. It must have made an almighty bang. You'd have heard it for miles."

"Well, they rebuilt it right away, seeing as it

was a prison wall, and it's probably stronger now than it ever was then. Of course, nothing lasts forever. It's overdue for repairs, crumbling all over the place. If you ever come across anyone who has experience with Victorian era limestone walls, can you get me his number? It seems the leak that brought down my ceiling was in the walls, not the roof, so I'd want to hire him first, but they want someone like that at work, too. The prison's applied for a grant to cover the costs, but there's no way they'll be able to spend the money if they can't find someone capable of doing the work."

"Well, I do know someone who did some repair work on my walls recently…" Catena bit her lip. "I'll see if he's available." How she'd explain Tor to Anemone, she didn't know, but if she didn't actually see him doing the repairs, it might be all right. Well, for her house, at least. When it came to the prison walls…she'd have to talk it over with Tor.

Anemone's eyes lit up. "If you can find me a

stonemason with the right skills, I'll make you dinner for a whole month, I'd be so grateful."

"No need for that." Though she wouldn't turn the offer down. Especially if she ended up living off the pittance of a PhD scholarship next year. "I don't even know if he'll be able to help."

"I'll cook him dinner, too!"

Catena had to laugh at that. "I'll ask him. Anyway, I should go. Leave you and your cat to enjoy each other's company..."

As if sensing her presence was required, the cat crossed the kitchen and began chowing down on something that smelled distinctly fishy.

Anemone rose. "Thank you. If you hear anything else, from your tradie or about the shoes, please let me know. Heaven knows I could do with some good luck, after the year I've had." Tears glistened in her eyes, but they didn't fall.

Sympathy swelled in Catena's chest. Tor should have been here, protecting Anemone.

She'd lost her husband and had the ceiling fall in…she definitely deserved a protector more than Catena. But from the little she'd learned about gargoyles, it didn't seem to work that way. Oh well, she'd ask him about that, too.

"Good night."

Catena headed home, but she hadn't even reached her own front door before she'd decided to spend more time talking to the lonely widow. The first thing she'd ask for was the recipe for that stew.

FORTY

"Tor? Are you here?" Catena called softly.

Of course he was. He'd been aware of her presence the moment she'd stuck her key in the front door, though he'd kept his distance when she visited her neighbour, just as she'd asked him to on her first visit, the night of the storm.

This was different, though. This was a summons. She needed him, and he could only obey.

"Of course, Miss Kelly. As ever, I am at your service." He stepped out of the wall and bowed low. A little clumsily, he had to admit, but he'd been a convict, not a courtier. Even if she didn't actually know that, she had to know he wasn't as high class as her.

She shook her head slowly. "A girl could get used to this. You're spoiling me, Tor, and I'm not sure it's a good thing."

Tor thought on her words for a long moment, before he said, "If I protect you, and do as you wish, I don't see how it can be a bad thing."

"Definitely spoiling me. And I'm about to ask you to do it again. I'm fast growing addicted to having you around."

Also not a bad thing, Tor thought but didn't say. If he had a choice between being dismissed back into the darkness or protecting Catena for the rest of her natural life, he'd choose her every time, and twice on Sundays.

She closed her eyes, as if her thoughts

pained her. "I couldn't sleep last night, worried about what Anemone found in her ceiling next door, and I'm scared tonight will be even worse, now I know even more about the practice. Can you…take a look around the house, in the ceiling cavity and between the walls, maybe even under the floorboards, and tell me if you find anything that shouldn't be there? Like…shoes, or a dead body or…anything else unpleasant I should know about."

Tor grinned. "I can assure you that in the course of my work – which is finished, by the way. Your house is completely repaired and without leaks, as good as new – I have not found any shoes or other items of clothing, and while there were a couple of rat skeletons that had likely been beneath the floor for decades, I disposed of these bodies in the wheeled rubbish receptacle behind your house. There are no dead bodies anywhere in your house."

Catena sagged with visible relief. "Tor, you

are a legend." She threw her arms around his neck and hugged him tightly.

Another awkward embrace. He refrained from patting her back this time, but he still felt bereft when it ended. Odd. Having her body close to his seemed like the most natural thing in the world, when he knew it was anything but.

She pulled away. "Sorry. You're not a hugger, are you? I should try to remember that better."

Tor coughed. "On the contrary, Miss Kelly. Should you feel the desire to hug me, you are welcome to do so, any time that you wish."

Her eyes narrowed. "This is part of the bit about being at my command, isn't it? The world has changed, and it's not about who gives the orders, at least not when it's about personal contact. If you don't want me to hug you, and I try to hug you, you get to tell me to fuck off. And I need to listen to you, and respect your wishes."

Tor took a long time to consider her words.

The world had indeed changed. The prison guards would not have agreed to fuck off. No, they would have laughed, chained him up, and lashed him, no matter what he wanted. Not only that, but Miss Kelly was completely the opposite to the warders in his past.

"Do I have your permission to speak frankly, Miss Kelly?" he asked.

Catena grinned. "Sure. I'm not sure I've been told to fuck off by a man with a sexy Scottish accent before. Have at it."

"Even if I was not your protector, my purpose to serve you, I would not dream of telling you to fuck off, as you say." He swallowed. Of course, being a gargoyle, it didn't moisten his throat in the slightest, but the reflex was still there. "If you wish to hug me, I welcome your embrace. I may be made of stone, living stone, but stone nonetheless, but I do feel, and I am particularly partial to the feeling of holding you in my arms." He paused, considering. "Perhaps it is partly because you are easier to protect when I hold you close."

Easier to kiss, too, if madness overcame him again. Though he would be careful to make sure it did not.

"So, let me get this straight. Yes, you like hugs, and no, we don't have any dead bodies in the house," she said.

Tor inclined his head. "Correct on both counts, Miss Kelly."

"My name is Catena, or Cat, like the little black creature Anemone has that smells like fish. Remember? Honorifics are for arseholes like the prime minister."

"I do not think I shall ever be in a position to address the prime minister, Miss...Catena."

"Let's hope we're both that lucky, then. Oh, and I almost forgot. All that talk of hugging distracted me. The leak at Anemone's place, the one that made her ceiling fall in. It's in the limestone wall outside her bathroom. I saw it when I went up into the ceiling. She said she was looking for an experienced stonemason to repair it, and seeing as you've been doing all this work around my house, I wondered if you'd be willing…"

"If it is part of the building in which you live, I would be only too happy to make the repairs, with your permission, for you did not wish me to enter your neighbour's home, and I must respect your wishes."

Catena wrinkled her nose. "No, I don't mean to ask you for a favour. Of course, I'm delighted that you've done all that work here, which I will pay you for, if and when I can. Free room and board for as long as you need, if nothing else. But Anemone's looking for a tradesman to pay to do the work. Plus, if she likes it, she works in a historic building, older than this one, that needs a lot of work done on it, and the owners are looking for a tradesman to do the repairs there, too. You wouldn't have to hang around here, protecting me from whatever stupid things I manage to get into. You could go back to building things that can stand the test of time. Important things."

It was on the tip of his tongue to say that

there was nothing more important to him than protecting her, but there was a yearning in his breast now for more than that. He wanted to keep doing what he'd done, to build her a home where she could be safe and happy and where he could live with her. Share her life, like…

His breath hissed out through his teeth. He didn't just want to protect her, he wanted to provide for her. To spend every day making her happy. Like a husband.

Which he could never be.

"I will pay this historic building a visit, and see if there is anything that can be done for it. Then, if I can repair it, you may tell your friend so."

Her shoulders sagged. Relieved again. "Would you? That would be wonderful. I don't think Anemone gets the final say in who does the repairs there, but if you can at least give her a quote. Shit, or a list of what needs to be done, seeing as neither of us knows much about the going rate for stonemasons or even limestone…"

"Where might I find it? I shall fly over tonight, and make my assessment."

"It's the walls of the old prison. She said something about how they fell down shortly after they were built, and they had all these witch marks on them to protect them. I was going to head up there maybe before work or on my lunch break tomorrow, to see if I could spot the carvings. It's too late now, after dark and all, not safe…"

The prison. The place he'd been so afraid of being trapped inside, he'd escaped, only to end up trapped here instead. Tor wasn't sure he could even enter the place without the memories overwhelming him again. He didn't imagine they'd still have the whipping post – as Catena had said, times had changed – but to stand there, with those walls looming over him, ready to bury him forever…

Tor swallowed again. He didn't dare ask, and yet he couldn't bear to do this without her. "We shall go tonight, together. I shall keep you safe, and we shall both see all that we wish to see." And if he went to pieces, the strength of her command to head home, and the need to protect her, would be enough to overrule his fear and force him to do what was needed.

Her eyes lit up. "You'll take me on a private tour of the prison walls tonight? With all your expert knowledge on how things were built back then? Fuck yes, let me get my coat, and let's go!"

Tor blinked. He had not expected her to agree so easily. At least, if he had to revisit the worst of his past, he'd get to do it with Catena in his arms. Nothing and no one bolstered his courage like she could.

FORTY-ONE

She might be padded in so many layers, the cold air would never get through, but still she could feel every muscle along Tor's torso, hard against her back. Toasty warm, too, not like stone at all. And when he flew…she felt so secure in his arms, her only thought of the drop below was how beautiful it looked from up here.

Gargoyle magic, she decided. It had to be.

For gargoyles to exist implied the existence of magic, and while she'd never believed in any of that stuff before, it was hard to deny that she was flying through the air in the arms of the most gorgeous gargoyle she'd ever seen.

Callie would never have called gargoyles ugly if she'd met Tor.

They landed in a patch of darkness outside the walls, where frosty grass crunched underfoot.

Tor stared at the wall for a moment, before he burst out laughing. He doubled over, slapping his thigh, until he rolled on the grass, still roaring with laughter.

"What is it?" She couldn't spy anything even remotely funny. Certainly nothing to warrant rolling on the ground, laughing her arse off.

"They built buttresses! Bloody buttresses! By God, I wish I'd been here to see it. I told them the walls would fall down unless they built buttresses. Did they? Tell me, did their walls fall down, like I told them they would?"

"Anemone said they fell down only a year

after they were built," Catena admitted.

This only made Tor laugh harder, slapping the ground so hard he left handprints in the sodden soil.

Without warning, he leaped to his feet. "Did they build them on the south wall, too? I have to see." He was half a metre in the air, flapping hard, before Catena could blink.

"Wait! You can't just leave me alone out here!" she cried, reaching up.

Tor grinned, leaned forward, then dived. He caught her around the waist before shooting up into the air, clearing the wall with its rusting razor wire and heading across the prison yard.

This was the part of the prison Catena couldn't bear. She squeezed her eyes shut, but still she saw the whipping post she'd hated, every school excursion to this horrible place. Anemone had told her it wasn't even the real one, soaked in the blood of so many prisoners, which was kept in a climate controlled room with the most delicate items in the museum collection. Convict clothes, whips, manacles, and a noose kept coiled in readiness for the gallows.

The rumble of Tor's laughter made her open her eyes again. They hovered near the top of the south wall, where she could see Fremantle spread out below, all the way to the night-dark sea.

"More buttresses?" she guessed.

"Yes! Look at them all! And covered in my mark, as though pretending it was my work would be enough to keep them standing! Fools!" He reached out and traced what looked like a six-petalled flower in a circle. "Here, and here, and over here, too!"

Even Catena could see what Anemone had meant. The wall and buttresses bore the same mark, every few metres. The marks were angled such that they would only be visible to someone working at heights, for they would be invisible from the ground.

Hidden marks, just like the shoes. They were everywhere. A city built on secret witchcraft, right in plain view. Someone should study this, and bring the hidden history to light so more people knew about it.

It was like the graffiti in Pompeii, innocent chalk markings on a wall, preserved for two millennia to tell the eruption's true date, and not the false one recorded in some old scholar's memoirs, many years afterward. Pliny, if she recalled correctly.

She wondered what other secrets this place hid. The prison, and all the other buildings convicts had built in Perth and Fremantle.

Maybe Tor would know.

"If this is your mark, but you didn't put it here…where can I see the real thing?" she asked.

"The Gatehouse. A proper gatehouse, this one is, like I'd build to guard the lower reaches of a castle. The angles must be perfect for ornate work like this one, which is why you must have a cut circle to compare it to." Tor flapped his wings – once, twice – and cleared the wall, setting them down on the road in front of the prison entrance. "There. Carved by my own hand, that was."

Catena could see the difference. Unlike the scratched marks on the wall, this one had been carved deep by someone with a steady, sure hand. This mark was not meant to be a secret, it was a signature.

"What does it mean?" she asked, running her fingers over it. It beggared belief that she could be standing here, speaking to the man who'd carved it almost two centuries earlier, but this was the sort of thing she'd dreamed about as a child. It was like finding out time travel really was possible.

"It means I made it. That it will stand strong against any storm. That it will not fall down around the occupants' ears because of shoddy work. It's not some plea for protection, scratching a magic rune to call the spirits down to hold the wall up, for the stones themselves are not up to the job. It says I made this, and it will stand."

Catena's mouth dropped open. Tor seemed to stand taller, his shoulders broader than they were before. Or maybe it was in the tilt of his head…he looked proud of his work, and so he should be, if his creations stood the test of time while the convict-built ones behind them blew over in the first storm.

What had it taken to break a man with such towering strength? She shuddered at the thought. Something terrible. Only something heart-breakingly awful could have shattered his hard-as-stone spirit, to make him bow his head so deeply he hadn't dared rise again until now.

Now, he was himself again, or almost.

This man's purpose was not to serve, though every inch of him screamed that he could and would protect.

Catena's mouth was dryer than the stones behind her. The Tor before her was everything she could have dreamed of in a man. A man who was more than she could ever hope for.

"Tor? What will I tell Anemone? When she asks me if you can fix the walls?"

She suspected she already knew what his answer would be, but she wanted to hear it from him.

"The only way to fix those crumbling walls is to tear them down and build them anew. Or let them fall into ruin, as they so clearly wish to do. Or, I could do as I have in your house, and painstakingly patch them, so they might stand for another century, but certainly no longer." He scrutinised her. "Are you cold, and impatient to return home? Have you seen enough of crumbling stonework, and silly superstition?"

Actually, she wanted to see more of it, for the seed of an idea was growing in the back of her mind, though she had yet to voice it. All in good time.

"I'm not cold, but I think we are done here. If you're ready to fly home, I'm happy to fly with you." Any time.

As Tor scooped her up and rose into the air, she wished they could fly everywhere together.

Then again, that would probably have the internet afire with videos of them, and one Moth Man video was more than enough.

She peered at the streets below them, searching for anyone with a camera pointed upward, but it was close to midnight on a weeknight, so no one was out to ruin her night.

So she just rested her head against Tor's broad chest, and enjoyed the ride.

FORTY-TWO

The roster had her working this weekend, so she paid her weekly visit to Maria on her day off, instead. Maria's mind was wandering more than usual today, so Catena just settled down to listen.

Then, when Maria paused to free her teeth from the caramel Tim Tam, Catena figured she may as well ask.

"What do you know about gargoyles,

Maria?"

A big swallow of coffee had Maria opening her mouth again, and wagging her finger, too.

"I bet you're thinking the only kind of gargoyles are the ones you see on medieval churches, aren't you? Well, you'd be wrong. Gargoyles go as far back as the earliest civilisations. They've been protecting buildings for as long as there were buildings. Egypt, the Middle East, even Pompeii had gargoyles, but they didn't look like those ugly things on top of the cathedral in Paris. Oh, no. They were fierce defenders, and they were lions and dragons with the faces of men. People believed they would rise up, actually come to life, and defend the buildings they stood guard over.

"I remember when I was working on a dig in Pompeii, a site that had been dug up by treasure hunters when the city was first discovered, then reburied. We, of course, were doing the thing properly, systematically. Anyway, the first night out, before we started work, we're all having a few drinks, saying what we hoped to find. It's a game you play, though more often than not, nobody actually wins, but when someone does, we all chip in and get the winner roaring drunk when the thing they wish for is discovered. I don't remember what I wished for – I didn't win, so it didn't matter.

"No, it was a local boy, home on summer holidays from university, I think, who had the strangest wish. He told this story about some barbarian woman, the daughter of a prosperous freedman, who set up a high class bathhouse in Pompeii. She took three lovers – a gladiator, an artist, and an engineer. Now, she loved all three equally, but each of the men wanted her to themselves. So one day, they played a game of chance, saying that the winner could have her. Well, they played, but before they could determine the winner, an earthquake toppled the house down on top of them, and all three of them died. When she got home, she was devastated, but, being a barbarian witch, she knew how to cast a spell to raise her lovers from the dead, and bind them to her forever. The catch was, she had to bury them beneath her house, before she could revive them, and there were only so many builders in Pompeii, and they were very much in demand after the earthquake. Being a freedman's daughter, and a barbarian to boot, she was way down the list, and she had to wait years for her turn. Finally, her house was rebuilt, and she planned a magnificent feast for the night she planned to revive her lovers. Only the volcano erupted, and she was forced to flee…leaving her lovers behind, still waiting for her to resurrect them.

"He'd grown up with the story, maybe he was even descended from that woman, but what he wanted to find was those three men's bodies."

Catena leaned forward, balanced on the edge of her seat. "So did you find them?"

Maria laughed. "Of course not! It was just a silly story. But every night, we came back to it. Arguing over which man we'd have chosen out of her three lovers. Whether you wanted a man who'd fill your house with beautiful art, or build you a house with the most modern and remarkable things, or the gladiator, all supple and athletic. I imagine the sex must have been amazing."

There was a reason Maria never had a roommate, though there was space in this room for two. She'd scandalised so many of the little old ladies with her open talk of sex that the nurses knew not to put anyone else in with her, or risk them having a heart attack.

"That reminds me of a ruined castle in the UK I worked at for a season. Don't remember which one it was. But they did have a little chapel with the roof missing. Down at the village pub, they told all sorts of stories about the castle. That the family's fortunes had been lost when the local lord went off on a crusade, leaving his wife to hold the fort, as it were. She did for a while, praying every day and every night in the little chapel, which apparently had a gargoyle on the roof.

"Anyway, one night she retired to the chapel, intending to have an all night prayer vigil for her husband. The next morning, when one of the servants came in to bring her her breakfast, both she and the gargoyle were gone. It turned out that instead of praying for her husband, she'd spent those nights sleeping with the gargoyle, until they decided to run away together. That's where I learned that gargoyles have a reputation as legendary lovers."

Catena felt her face grow hot. If the lady's gargoyle had looked like Tor, no wonder she couldn't resist. Especially with her husband off killing people in the name of religion.

Maria sighed. "You know, if I have one regret in life, it's that I never got to seduce a gargoyle. And I never got seduced by one. When she's old enough, I must tell my goddaughter that. She should try to live without regrets and, if the opportunity arises, she should seize life with both hands, and seduce the gargoyle."

Tor? Maria thought she should seduce Tor?

"What do you mean, Maria?"

Maria squinted at her. "I don't know you. Who are you? Why does no one visit me any more? I want to see my goddaughter. Don't you touch my Tim Tams, they're her favourite, you know." Maria's fingers clawed at the empty biscuit packet, clutching it to her chest.

Catena sighed, but summoned a smile anyway. "Have a lovely weekend, Maria. I'll see you next week. There's a new Persian restaurant around the corner from me, and they make the most amazing sweets. I'll have to bring you some to taste." She kissed Maria's cheek, then rose to leave.

She was still shaking her head by the time she got to the car park. So many wild stories — and how much of them were true? That Maria had heard such tales on her travels, Catena didn't doubt, but whether there was any truth in them…

Seduce the gargoyle. As if she needed any encouragement. Tor already featured in her dreams on a nightly basis. To have him truly in her bed…

No, it'd never happen. That was for crusader ladies in castles and wealthy Roman matrons with their own bathhouses. Or romance heroines in books.

But she could always dream…

FORTY-THREE

"Hey, can you meet me in my office when you get a minute?" Callie asked, standing in the library foyer, leaning on one of the gates that screeched if anyone tried to leave the library with a book they hadn't borrowed.

Dread curdled the coffee in Catena's belly. "What is it?" It had to be bad news.

"I hit the motherlode on those shoes of yours, but this stuff is dark. Lose your lunch dark, and that's just the stuff in English. In some of my Latin texts…that stuff will give you nightmares. Best I tell you everything in my office, with the door closed. Don't want any of the students overhearing, and deciding to try things out over the holidays. The best thing that might happen is they get arrested."

It couldn't be any worse than Maria telling her to sleep with a gargoyle, could it?

"Sure," Catena said. "I'll pop in when Emily, the girl working the evening shift, arrives."

The afternoon passed swiftly, sped on by the rash of students interested in Moth Men once more. As if this second wave of conspiracy chasing students had been too deep in study to notice the viral video when it first released, and it was doing the rounds a second time. Unless there was a new video…

Catena paused mid-breath, about to tell the student in front of her where to find the nearest fiction bookshop, to see Emily, one of the casual assistants, swan through the doors with a wave and a smile.

Emily waited for the student to depart before she asked, "So where are the Moth Man books, exactly?"

Catena swatted at her half-heartedly with the nearest notebook. "You know the answer to that. Same as last time."

"Aww…but he looks so real in the video! So dark and mysterious, and those moves! I wouldn't say no to a dance with him," Emily teased.

Catena shook her head. "Tell you what. If you can catch a Moth Man, we can set him up in the corner as a special exhibit, for all the students to stare at."

"You'd have to offer a reward better than the one on offer for him for that. I mean, a year's free coffee is pretty hard to top."

"I get free coffee from the university. I'm good," Catena said, lifting her bag onto her shoulder. "There's a stack of books still waiting in the returns slot. Shelve them if you have time, but it's okay if you leave them for me to do in the morning. I'm off."

They said their goodbyes and Catena was indeed off, across the courtyard to Callie's office.

She knocked tentatively.

"I'm busy! Vitally important research project on a deadline!" Callie called.

"I'll come back tomorrow, then," Catena said, turning to walk away.

The door flew open. Callie grabbed her arm and yanked her inside, before slamming the door behind her.

Catena disentangled herself from Callie's grip. "Vitally important project on a deadline, huh?"

Callie shrugged. "Well, it could be vitally important. I won't know unless I've translated it all, will I? So far it's all about how to summon demons and other magical servants, by opening doorways to other realms but no word on how to shut them again once you have. I think it's important to know how to close the gates of hell, don't you?"

"Who's this translation project for?"

Callie grinned impishly. "You, of course. You did ask for stuff on foundation sacrifices. Doorways are just the beginning."

Catena threw herself into Callie's visitor chair. "Okay, hit me with it."

"All right, then! Well, the surface stuff you've probably found already. There's plenty of articles in the literature, and even a couple of theses. All recent, in the last decade or so. So if you're looking for something to put in a research or grant proposal for, you're in luck. It's kind of like the wild west out there – stake your claim, and hope it pans out."

Do her PhD on shoes? Callie had to be dreaming to even suggest it.

"This is just a favour for my neighbour, and maybe a bit of my own presence of mind. I mean, we live in the same building, which is divided into two apartments. So if her half's cursed, you can be pretty sure mine is, too."

Callie clapped her hands together in ghoulish delight. "Oh, you don't know the half of it! Curses, my sweet summer child, are nothing compared to the dark magic I've dug up. In fact..."

The door swung open, and one of the theology professors stood there, his glasses halfway down his nose as he peered down at his phone. "Callie, I need you to do some research for me. There's some sort of creature called a Moth Man, and all my students are asking about it. I must know which level of hell it hails from." He glanced up at her, as though expecting her to answer him on the spot.

Callie rose from her seat and crossed the office to stand in front of him, doorknob in hand. "The bullshit level, Christian. Moth Men don't exist. Now, if you'll excuse me, I was in the middle of an important meeting..."

Professor Christian held out his phone, waving it around like it was an incense burner at Easter mass. "But there's a video, and it's clearly a winged demon dancing! How can I have any credibility with my students if I can't identify all the demons in hell?"

"I can't help you, Christian. I'm not an expert in demons, after all. Just the Latin lecturer. Now, if you want any texts you find in your research translated, then I might be able to help you, but I'm very busy at the moment, so you'll have to wait for a spot to open up in my schedule, same as everyone else."

Professor Christian eyed Catena balefully. "Aren't you the junior librarian? You must be able to help me find out about these things."

Now she remembered where she'd met Professor Christian before. He'd come into the library, demanding she provide him with books on this new gang style modern demonic summoning ritual. It had taken the better part of an hour for her to work out he meant Gangnam Style, and an even more excruciating forty-five minutes showing him how to access the music video on one of the library computers.

As if the heavens had heard the prayer she hadn't yet even put into words, Catena's phone buzzed. She didn't even glance at the screen.

Even if it was some foreign scammer pretending to be from a bogus government department, threatening to come and arrest her, it would be an improvement on dealing with Professor Christian.

Catena grabbed her things and made a dash for the door. "I really need to take this. I'll talk to you later, Callie!" she shouted as she beat a hasty retreat.

It was a foreign number, she realised. Oh well, she could just hang up on them, mid-threat. "Hello?" she ventured.

"Cat! It's so good to hear your voice!"

Catena blinked. "Is that Sybil?"

"That's me! Fresh from the frozen wastes of the Arctic, back in civilisation for a little while before they send me back to site with the next load of supplies. Would you believe that in this day and age, we have to bring everything in via donkey?"

As Sybil began to describe the day to day workings on the dig she'd been volunteering on for the North Pole summer, in a pit of melting permafrost that had been frozen for more than a thousand years.

"It sounds amazing," Catena admitted. It was the sort of adventure Maria would have worked on.

"I haven't even told you the best part! I've…met someone…and I'll probably be staying for another season, to see what else we can find. I'm learning so much," Sybil gushed. "How about you? Have you decided on a PhD project yet, or did Alethea talk you into joining her company as a consultant instead?"

"I'm finalising my project proposal this week. I definitely want to do my PhD next year, and no, Alethea hadn't managed to talk me into digging up dead bodies with her. Did you know their latest project was digging up an old colonial cemetery?" Catena shuddered. She'd been worried about maybe finding bodies buried in her house. Digging up a whole cemetery full of skeletons was way too creepy.

"Well, you know that's the holy grail up

here. Dead bodies. Frozen ones. They're hoping to find another ice mummy like Otzi. My friend says we have a good chance of finding one, too, because it was an ancient trading and raiding route. Thor knows so much about Viking history…"

Catena shook her head. So her new boyfriend was a fellow archaeologist. Maria had warned her never to get involved with her colleagues. Well, seriously, anyway. Some of the stories she'd told about the guys she'd dated or slept with would have curled her mother's hair, if she'd known about them. But she'd never been serious about any of them. Just a bit of fun, she'd said.

"Anyway, what about you? Have you met anyone yet? And what's this I hear about you having a major moth problem? I tried to watch the video, but I only saw a few seconds of his moves before the video froze. The internet connection here keeps dropping out. It might feel like civilisation after the dig site, but it's really just a few storage rooms and a lab, on the outskirts of a tiny town. So, are you going to tell me about him?"

Even on the other side of the world, Sybil had heard of the Moth Man.

"There's nothing to tell, really. Just a silly video of a guy in a coat they're making out to be a monster. He's not, honestly. He's the sweetest, most chivalrous guy I've ever met. He's…" No, she couldn't tell her about Tor. "We're just friends," she finished lamely.

"Uh huh. Sure. Just like me and Thor. I want to know where he learned to dance like that. I expect to meet him when I get home. Or we can video call when we're done. I want to hear every single detail." While Sybil paused, Catena heard indistinct voices in the background. Then Sybil was back. "Sorry, Cat, I have to go. Thor said one of the artefacts is missing, and it's really important. Talk later. Bye."

"Bye," Catena echoed, but Sybil was already gone.

That video really had gone viral, if Sybil had

seen it.

It wasn't until she was halfway home that the professor's words hit her – a video with a winged demon dancing. Wasn't that what Emily had said, too? Wanting to dance with the Moth Man? Even Sybil had said something about the Moth Man's moves. The video that had caused all that trouble hadn't involved dancing – just her, Tor and that busker in the dark.

This new flurry of interest must mean there was a new video.

Catena's steps quickened, beating war drums on the pavement. Tor was going to be in deep trouble when she got home.

FORTY-FOUR

The café across the road was packed again tonight, with people spilling out onto the footpath. Catena huffed out a disapproving breath. Didn't they have homes to go to? Who wanted coffee this late in the evening, anyway?

She crossed the road to avoid them, glad to see the roadworks were finished and the fences were down, so traffic could flow again. In the flickering lights of Tayla's shop sign, she dug through her bag for her keys.

"Miss! Miss!"

"Do you know the Moth Man?"

"Was the Moth Man dancing for you?"

"What's the Moth Man's name, miss?"

Fuck.

No more fences meant there was nothing to stop the crowd from crossing the road to surround her, blocking her access to her own front door.

There had to be a new video. She was going to kill Tor when she got inside. "Tor," she cursed under her breath.

A breath of wind ruffled her coat, before something warm and solid took its place.

"Now, people, it's late, and the lady wants to go inside. Make space for the lady!" The authoritative bellow could belong to no one else.

A curtain of dark wool appeared between Catena and the crowd. Warm wool, draped over a pair of powerful arms that pushed their way effortlessly through the people, clearing her path.

"Thank you, Tor," she breathed.

"Only doing my job," he said. "Now, do you have your keys?"

She held them up, still tightly clutched in her shaking hand. Then she got a hold of herself, and put the key in the lock instead. She cracked the door open, then squeezed through, while Tor shielded her from view.

It seemed a hellish eternity, but could only have been a few seconds, before she and Tor stood alone in the foyer, separated from the crowd by the closed leadlight door.

Only then did Catena dare to breathe again. She wanted nothing more than to throw herself in Tor's arms and stay there until she stopped shaking, but they still had an audience outside, peering avidly through the coloured glass panes.

Besides, he might have rescued her from those reporters, but she couldn't forget he was the reason they were out there. He'd gotten caught on camera again, and she wouldn't rest until he understood why he couldn't risk that.

"Upstairs. Now," she bit out through gritted teeth, leading the way.

FORTY-FIVE

"Come with me," Catena said, and Tor was only happy to follow. Instead of the kitchen, she headed for her office, the room with the small screen. She pressed some buttons and the screen flickered to life. More buttons, on the flat panel on the desk this time, until a picture of this building appeared, the gargoyle statue perched pensively on top.

"This aether of yours is truly remarkable,"

Tor said.

"It's called the internet, and today it's a curse, I promise you. And I don't want to hear another word from you until after we have watched this godforsaken video, when the only thing I want to hear is your explanation why."

Cryptic instructions, but not so difficult that he could not understand and obey. Still feeling somewhat triumphant about successfully rescuing her downstairs, he said, "As you wish, Miss Kelly."

"Oooh!" She stabbed at the little triangle that made a movie begin to move, and move it did.

It was this house, at night, just as it was now. Then the whole picture shifted, as though someone hard turned their head to look right. Something was moving about on top of the ramparts that marked the edge of the roof. It was the size of a man, but had wings, much like his. The longer he stared, the more certain he became.

"That is a gargoyle on your roof," he said.

The gargoyle began to dance in the most outlandish fashion, shaking his behind and wiggling about like some sort of savage, then giving a little jump and doing it all again. It was most peculiar.

The movie ended.

Catena turned to him, with fire in her eyes. "Now, I want you to tell me why on Earth you were dancing the bloody Macarena on my roof while someone filmed you from the street below!"

Tor couldn't stop himself. He burst out laughing. "Miss Kelly, I could not dance like that if I took lessons every day for a year. I could not dance a simple reel at Hogmanay without getting my feet tangled together and toppling over. I swear to you, that dancing gargoyle on your roof is not me."

She stared at him for a long moment. Finally, her shoulders relaxed and she nodded. "When I first heard there was a new video, I was afraid it was going to be of us flying to the prison the other night. I hadn't actually seen it until now. I mean, a naked dude dancing isn't much better, but at least I'm not in it. And…you're telling the truth? You truly can't move like that?"

Tor shook his head. "Most assuredly not. I have never waggled my behind in such a way in my life!"

Catena gave a sad smile. "Pity," he thought he heard her say, before she headed out of the room.

FORTY-SIX

Sunday lunchtime saw Catena yawning behind the loans desk at the library, wishing she could have slept longer. She didn't regret staying up late, watching a Stargate marathon with Tor, but maybe she should have gone to bed a little earlier. He could have kept watching them without her – it wasn't like he needed sleep, and she'd definitely seen them all before.

But it was fun to watch them with someone

who was seeing them for the first time, to be there to explain things that referenced history Tor had slept through, and…and…

The more time she spent with him, the more she liked him. Really like liked him. He wasn't entirely perfect (he did like to hog the remote control), but he was about as close to it as any man she'd ever met.

She had to wonder, though, what with him being made of stone and all…could he feel desire, like she did? He obviously had all the right bits for a physical relationship with someone, but…did they actually work? And would he want to…with her?

She wanted to kiss him again. Without an audience of rabid reporters, and not with her feet so frozen she could barely feel them. She wanted to kiss him somewhere they could…do more, if that's what he wanted. She'd given up denying what she wanted. Tor, naked, in her bed, preferably all night.

And…this was not the place to be thinking about Tor naked. Not with students about.

The day crawled. The few students in the library seemed perfectly happy to keep their distance, studying or researching or whatever they were doing at the tables near the shelves. Catena had lost count of the number of times she'd needed to shake herself awake, after nearly falling asleep on the loans desk.

Finally, the last of the students left and she did one last lap around the library, switching things off, before she headed home.

The grinding vibration of her phone on the desk was audible even from the far side of the room. Catena hurried to answer it, but she was too late. She pulled up the number – Maria's nursing home – and hit redial.

After what felt like an eternity, someone finally picked up.

"Hi, this is Catena Kelly. I had a missed call from you. If this is about me missing my visit to Maria this afternoon, don't worry, I came on Thursday instead because I had to work today. I'll be back again next Sunday, just like every other week – "

"Miss Kelly. Yes. This is about Maria Rennie. I am sorry to say she passed away this morning."

"She...what?" Catena couldn't have heard right. Maria had been in almost perfect health. Her mind was failing, yes, but the rest of her...this had to be a mistake.

"She passed away this morning, some time after breakfast. The staff did not know until this afternoon because there is sickness here and they were so busy cleaning and caring for the sick patients, that they did not find Miss Maria until it was too late."

"How...how did she die?"

"The doctor said she had a stroke, Miss Kelly. She would not have felt any pain. She looked like she was asleep, so the staff thought..."

Which explained why they hadn't called her until now. Poor Maria had been dead in her bed for hours, and no one had noticed. Catena wasn't sure if she wanted to scream or cry or both.

"I'm just leaving work now. I'll be right there," Catena said.

"You can't come here, Miss Kelly. We are under quarantine. There is a sickness, many of our patients are sick. No visitors allowed."

"But she can't just stay there. She deserves…" Something. Catena had never organised a funeral before. She didn't know the first thing about them.

"The funeral director will come to collect her. They will contact you to arrange a date. She made arrangements already, her files says. She had funeral insurance. As her next of kin, of course you can discuss any changes you wish to make with the funeral director…"

Go against Maria's last wishes? Catena almost laughed. Maria had wanted to be cremated, and her ashes scattered somewhere that no one would dig them up and make up stories about her. No archaeologist was going to handle her remains without her permission, she'd said many times, and anyone who was complicit in letting such a thing happen…she'd haunt them so thoroughly, she'd made Tutankhamen's curse look like a blessing.

Catena mumbled some sort of response, about coming to collect Maria's things when they were open for visitors again, and ended the call.

Maria, the godmother who'd been like a second mother and cool aunt and best friend and mentor all rolled into one, was gone, and Catena's life would never be the same without her.

She wasn't sure how she got home, or how long she sat on the sofa, staring at the dark screen where she'd watched all those Stargate episodes with her godmother, before Tor found her.

Being the perfect man he was, he didn't ask questions. He simply opened his arms wide for her.

Catena dove into his embrace and burst into tears.

FORTY-SEVEN

Catena left a final message on Maria's social media accounts, telling her friends and colleagues the time and date for her funeral. They'd just about blown up the internet with all the messages – condolences, regrets that they couldn't attend, and a whole load of memories about how wonderful Maria had been.

All the stories Maria had told about the

archaeological digs she'd been on around the world were just the tip of the iceberg. Everyone had their own memories of Maria, and, more than once, Catena found herself laughing out loud before she remembered that her godmother was gone and laughter was hardly appropriate right now.

Maria had insisted on having her funeral in a function room at the crematorium, with a non-religious celebrant, with as little food as possible after to deter the vultures, or at least that's what she'd said. Catena wasn't sure who she'd meant, but every seat in the function room had been filled, so there'd been people standing up the back.

The funeral home had brought out enough food for everyone at the wake, with so much left over, Catena had been forced to take a lot of it home.

Not that she could bring herself to eat anything. Nor had she been able to write a proper speech that did her godmother justice.

Every time she'd sat down to try to write

something, she'd managed little more than a sentence or two before dissolving into tears.

Luckily, enough of Maria's colleagues, some of them students she'd mentored who were professors in their own right now, were more than capable of giving good speeches, telling Maria's story with more enthusiasm than Catena could muster.

In the end, she'd had to stand up beneath the projector screen, ready to play the slideshow of photos she'd scanned from Maria's collection, and said all she could: "Maria was my godmother. I loved every day I got to spend with her, and I will miss her every day from now on that I can't."

The slideshow flickered on the screen above Maria's coffin, while people came up to lay their flowers on the polished box.

Catena wasn't the only one crying by the time they all wandered out to where the food was set out for the wake.

Most of the people didn't stay long afterwards, and she was soon left with just her family and a few stragglers. Her eyes too blurred by tears to see straight any more, Catena just wanted the ordeal to be over. Maria was gone. She'd said her goodbyes, and now all that was left was the big, gaping hole in her heart where her godmother used to be.

Her mother packed up the leftovers to take back to Maria's apartment – Maria's no longer, with the reading of her will set to happen next week – and guided Catena home.

FORTY-EIGHT

A plate of cakes and pastry parcels of who knew what sat in front of Catena, untouched. Her parents had long since finished theirs and her brother was serving up his third helping, mostly dessert. It felt wrong to eat leftovers from Maria's funeral feast on Maria's own dining table, without Maria herself to preside over the meal.

Catena usually ate at the kitchen bench or in

the lounge, in front of the TV, because of how many memories this table held.

It didn't hold the same weight for the rest of her family, though. They treated it like their own dining table at home. Dad and Archie had even begun a heated argument, just like they would at any normal Sunday lunch.

"She should have called a priest to administer Last Rites, and the funeral should have been in a church! These things might not matter as much when you're alive, but when you're about to meet your maker, they mean a lot more!"

Archie shook his head. "You sound like such a hypocrite, Dad. You can't just pick up religion when it suits you and ignore it when it's inconvenient. It's all about living your life as best you can in accordance with church teachings. A few blessings and prayers after you're dead aren't going to do much for your soul if you weren't a good person during your life."

"Don't you dare say your sister's godmother

wasn't a good person! I mean, sure, she spent most of her time digging up religious idols and temples to every pagan god under the sun, but she was a good Catholic, even if she never went to church! She deserved a proper send off, with a priest!"

Maria might have been born Catholic, but she'd long since given up on belief in any single deity, Catena knew. Maria had once joked that she almost looked forward to dying, because then she'd finally find out who was right about the afterlife. Or if it was everyone, and she'd get to talk to the deities whose religious relics she'd spent her life digging up. Imagine actually asking Osiris how he'd become the god of the underworld! Or finding out they really were a race of alien parasites who built the pyramids as landing platforms for their spaceships…

"She's going to be cremated anyway! What's the point of doing the whole thing properly with a priest if her body's going to be burned? No, you should die the way you lived. One way or the other. No saving someone at the last minute, like some sort of action movie. That's not what we learned in Sunday school…"

"But she didn't even let her have Last Rites! That's one of the sacraments – it's sacrilege to deny her that!"

"She refused to have it!"

"She couldn't refuse anything – she had a stroke, and died pretty much instantly. No one had the chance to ask her, so it should've been given anyway. It's the least she could have done."

As the shouting grew louder, Catena felt the irresistible urge to run. But where could she run to? This was her house, and they were here. It was already dark outside. It wasn't like she could safely run out into the street…

"Hello, what's all the fuss about?"

Tor stood in the kitchen doorway, his arms folded across his chest, beneath the wool coat that hid his wings.

Catena wanted to run to him and kiss him for his perfect timing.

"Okay, I grant you that maybe Last Rites might have been in order, just in case, but she'd planned and paid for the funeral well before she died. She made her decision, and we have to respect that, even if we don't agree with it," Archie continued, oblivious.

"But she was WRONG!" Dad exploded.

"I beg your pardon, gents, but there are ladies present. Perhaps you should take this argument outside," Tor said. "Sort it out between yourselves like men. The ladies don't need to bear witness to such unpleasantness."

Archie snorted. "Cat's no lady. And Mum…"

"You watch your tongue when you're talking about your mother, or I'll take you outside and thrash you like my Dad used to do to me!"

"Gentlemen!" Tor's bellow silenced them both for a second.

"Will you introduce us to your friend, Cat?" Mum asked.

Catena knew that look. "Mum, Dad, Archie,

this is Tor. He's a consultant, come to visit from Scotland. He's an expert in Victorian era stonework, and he's advising the Fremantle Prison on some upcoming restoration work. He's staying with me because I had a spare room."

Not for the reason that had Mum's eyes sparkling.

Dad squinted suspiciously at him. "Tor. That's a strange name."

Tor produced a polite smile. "An old family name, in fact. I'm Torstan Stone. Like Miss Kelly said, people call me Tor." He reached out to shake hands with Dad, then Archie.

Catena had to hide her smile as she caught Archie's wince at what looked to be an extremely firm handshake.

Dad would not be deterred, though. Ever a dog with a bone, worrying it to death. "I still say it was all done wrong. What she should have done…"

Tor coughed. "Actually, Miss Kelly has gone to great pains this week to ensure her godmother's wishes were respected in all things. A terrible time for her to have a houseguest, but her hospitality through it all has been impeccable. I could not help but observe how well she has organised everything. Agonising over every detail, though it seemed Dr Maria had planned it all quite thoroughly. Seeing as this was Dr Maria's home and is now Miss Kelly's, you should show both ladies the respect they deserve in honouring their decisions beneath their own roof, or I must insist you leave."

Despite standing on the other side of the table from them, he appeared to loom over both Dad and Archie. Quite alarmingly.

Dad had never been one to back down from a fight. "Now, I don't know who you think you are, Tor Stone, but this is my daughter's house, and I won't be ordered about by any houseguest of hers. So you can just…"

Tor grinned. "Mr Kelly, I would be only too happy to take this disagreement outside. For as we are both her guests, it seems only polite not to disturb the peace of her home so…"

A horrible image of Tor and Dad squaring up for a fistfight popped into Catena's head. Tor would flatten him. She couldn't allow this.

"How about you boys take the rest of the cakes to the lounge room?" Catena burst out. "I'm sure there's a football match on, or a movie you can watch. Maria has…had…every single Bond film on DVD…" She shot a desperate look of entreaty at Tor. "You can show them how to use the player and the TV, right?"

"If you're sure, Miss Kelly," he said.

"Yes. It's too cold to go outside tonight," she insisted.

"Very well."

Tor followed Dad and Archie into the lounge, where they were already debating the merits of Moore, Connery and Brosnan. Neither of them professed to be a fan of Daniel Craig, though they'd watched his movies often enough.

"I'll help you with the washing up," Mum

said, reaching for the plates the men had left behind.

Catena wanted to follow the men, to make sure Tor didn't say anything too revealing without her being there to explain it away, but she recognised Mum's tone and there was no refusing her.

In the kitchen, where the hiss of hot water and the clink of dishes in the sink drowned out the sounds of conversation in the other room, Mum raised her eyebrows.

"He's a colleague. He's just staying with me, Mum, nothing more," Catena protested.

"He's a remarkably chivalrous one. So how long have you been...colleagues, then?"

She made it sound like they'd been sharing crazy tantric sex, not just sharing Maria's house and one heart-stopping kiss.

"I only met him a week or two ago, Mum, and he needed a place to stay. That's all." Sadly.

Mum turned the water off with a firm flick. "Well, I like him, and I hope he stays with you for a while."

It was on the tip of her tongue to tell her mum she hoped the same thing, but there was no point getting Mum's hopes up. Worse, she'd start interrogating Tor, trying to work out what chance she had of getting grandchildren soon, and there was no way Catena wanted him subjected to that.

No, she owed him very grateful thanks for intervening when he had. More than words, but what else would he accept?

Much later, when her family had finally left after consuming every bite of leftover food, she turned to tell him.

Warm arms closed around her. "Forgive my impertinence, Miss Kelly, for I did not know your godmother well, but I believe she would have been proud of you today. You honoured her wishes exactly as she wanted, and that is the best testament of respect to her memory that anyone could ever offer. Even in the face of your family's disapproval, you stood firm. I am in awe of your courage. I could not have defied my father so easily, and it is clear that you inherited his air of authority, even if you refrain from using it. I am honoured to be your protector."

Was it wrong that she wanted him to be more than just her protector? So much more…

FORTY-NINE

Catena withdrew from his embrace, a polite smile upon her face as though it had been the most acceptable thing in the world, instead of a liberty he should not have taken. "Thank you for everything tonight, Tor. I'm not sure how I would have got through it without you."

"I am honoured to be of service, Miss Kelly."

"I am curious, though. You wouldn't have

actually fought my father, would you? Or duelled with him or whatever? Because we don't do that sort of thing any more," Catena said.

Tor laughed. "Had your father stepped outside with me, or your brother, there might have been some friendly fisticuffs, but no more, I'm sure. I am as good a boxer as I am a dancer, I'm afraid. Clumsy as an ox, people have called me, and they'd be right. I lumber about in the ring too slowly to avoid a more nimble boxer's blows. Your relatives would have landed a few punches, my stone skin would have protected me from injury, and we would have declared them the winners, and become friends. Just as modern men did in your movie about underground boxing clubs."

Catena blinked. "Which movie is that?"

Tor winked. "The first rule is that we do not speak of it. The second rule…"

"Ah. *Fight Club*. Yes. Okay, maybe men haven't changed that much, then."

Tor grinned. "Indeed we have not. I must

thank you for permitting me to attend your family party this evening. I can scarcely remember a time when I was just another man among men, free to do as I pleased, and not bound to duty. Even before I came here, I had a duty to my family, my father. Work hard and one day, you will be free, he told me, even upon his death bed. And when I came here, it was the same. I had to work hard, but in the hope that through hard work, I would be free. Now, the work is far less hard. In fact, my duty to protect you is so pleasant it scarcely feels like work. But even if it was not, if you wandered into danger far more readily than you do, I would not mind a jot, for I have only to remind myself that work will set me free, and – "

"What did you say?" Catena gripped the chair so tightly her knuckles had gone white. "Work will set you free?"

Tor inclined his head. "Of course. Everyone knew this. If you work hard enough, obey the orders you are given, one day you will be free to be your own man, answering to no one."

Catena shook her head. "It's a lie, Tor. A lie told by rich men who exploited everyone else, who still exploit everyone else, because their power is based on everyone else working hard and obeying orders, until they work themselves to death trying to win a future they can't possibly win, because the men with money in power won't let them."

"Oh, no, Miss Kelly. My father never lied in his life. He was a stickler for the truth. He would not have lied to me about something so important." If she were a man, he would call her out right now for insulting his father so.

She bit her lip. "I'm sure your father believed what he said, but that doesn't make it any less of a lie. It makes it worse, actually, because someone lied to him so thoroughly they made him believe it, and pass it on to you. God, it was even written on the gates of Auschwitz, the work camp where prisoners worked themselves to death in the war, that work would set them free, and that was the biggest lie of all. Because the only way those poor people got freed, at least before the war ended, was to die."

Her eyes blazed. "I'd like to meet whoever it was who bound you to protect me, Tor, because I want to kick his arse all the way back to where he came from. He lied to you, he enslaved you, and whatever he promised you, when he told you hard work would set you free, that was a lie, too, because he had no intention of ever setting you free. Unless gargoyles can die, because…oh, fuck, I wish Maria were still here. She'd help me kick his arse, because this isn't fair. You deserve to be your own man, like anyone else."

Tor shook his head. No. "Not yet. I don't deserve that yet. But one day…"

She slammed her hand down on the table. "Don't you argue with me, Torstan Stone. You've been brainwashed all your life into believing this bullshit. And it is bullshit, I promise you. Because I swear, I will find a way to set you free, and then you will see what you do deserve. It's everything those lying arseholes promised you, and more. I'll find a way, Tor, I promise."

He wanted to believe her. Hope rose like a bubble in his chest, that her words could be true. He hardly dared believe it, but when he looked into the righteous fire in her eyes, he didn't dare doubt her, either.

It was an honour to protect her. Not because it was his duty, or because he was bound to do it. It was an honour, because she was a fierce, avenging angel, who did not need to fight for someone as lowly as him, but she did it anyway.

"From your lips to God's ears, Miss Kelly," he said. For surely not even God could ignore the voice of his fiercest angel.

FIFTY

Returning to work was surreal. Nothing had changed, and yet…everything had.

"Where have you BEEN?" Callie exclaimed in the lunch room. "You bolted out of my office like there were demons chasing you — though, I wouldn't put it past Christian to put them up to it, he knows enough about them — and then no one's seen you for a whole week!"

Catena swallowed. It would get easier, but

right now she had to fight to get the words out. "I had to take some personal leave. My godmother died. I'm…I was her closest relative, so I had to make all the funeral arrangements. And then there was her will…she left everything to me. Her house, everything. I've been living there anyway, while she was in the nursing home, but now she's gone, it's…weird, wandering around a house full of her things, and knowing she'll never come back for them, because I'll never see her again."

"Well, unless you can raise the dead. Sorry, bad joke. I'm so sorry for your loss. That fucking sucks. I mean, I saw in the news that Maria Rennie had died, they had a full eulogy and everything, but I forgot that she was your godmother. No wonder you went into archaeology – she went everywhere, discovered so much! I bet she bequeathed you a whole bunch of artefacts, too. Stuff thousands of years old, imbued with all sorts of ancient curses…"

Catena shook her head. "Maria always said what she discovered belonged to everybody. She didn't want to take things home, because she couldn't preserve them properly at home. She took pictures of everything, though – there's a whole bookcase full of slides. And every file had a picture of her with the dig teams, all the different places…"

"Ooh, speaking of digging things up, you ran out on me the other day before I could get to the good stuff. My office. Now."

"I can't. I have to open the library in five minutes."

Callie made a rude noise and waved her hand. "Let Lillian do it. She's already there, and it won't hurt her. She didn't know when you'd be back, so I don't think she's expecting you today. So come with me and we can pick up where we left off when Christian so rudely interrupted."

Part of Catena wanted to go to the library and relieve Lillian, slipping back into her normal life as if nothing had happened. But this was important, partly because it might give her an angle on a possible PhD project and partly because of her promise to Tor.

So she stirred an extra spoon of sugar into her coffee, and followed Callie.

She took the guest chair again, while Callie spun around in her desk chair to face her. "Right. I told you all the dry stuff – the literature, and those theses – which I'm sure you found on your own. But it's the more obscure references where it gets really good. The first records date back to Ancient Rome, where one of the scholars describes the ancient Germanic peoples using captured enemies as foundation sacrifices. They'd bury the bodies under the lintel of their houses, ready to rise again to defend them when the next enemy attacked. Kind of like Romans raising armies among their conquered peoples, to go out and conquer more people…only the supernatural sort. Of course, while this Roman scholar saw the bodies being buried, he never saw them actually rise again and fight, so he chalked it up to superstition and that was that.

"Then I found some dark spell books, or at least that's what they're supposed to be. According to the first few pages, they're the copy of a collection of earlier works based on the spells and rituals of Viking witches. Vikings being the seagoing descendants of some of those ancient Germanic peoples, and some Slavic ones, too, I figured it was worth a look, and I wasn't disappointed. Horrified, yes, and a bit nauseated, because these witches were into some seriously dark shit, but they actually laid out how they did the sacrifices. In among a whole lot of dark rituals for summoning demons and protectors and plagues and storms. Oh, and one to make a volcano erupt. Of course, you need a volcano for that one, and a whole bunch of weird ingredients. Plus a sacrifice. This book is big on human sacrifice. Though technically for the volcano one, you're supposed to kill a vampire."

Catena laughed. "Don't tell me you believe vampires exist now?"

"Of course not. And I'm not sure these witches did, either. They didn't call it a vampire, but a wretch who had drunk the blood of his own flesh and blood, so maybe they actually meant a cannibal. So, maybe it was actually a good deterrent for cannibalism. Don't eat the dead bodies, even if you're starving, or the witches will throw you in a volcano, and then it'll be worse for everybody."

They both laughed at that.

"Okay, but…the bit about summoning protectors and things. Can you tell me more about that?" Catena asked.

"Funny you should ask, because that's the bit that matches the Roman scholar's account, though it goes into way more detail. Okay, let me find the exact page and I'll paraphrase for you. Here it is. There's a lot of steps. First, you have to find an enemy. The stronger, the better, because they make better undead defenders. Then you make him drink some sort of herbal tea. I couldn't translate the ingredients, but whatever they are, they're supposed to put him to sleep. Then you cut out his heart…yep, his actual heart…or, wait. Maybe you don't cut out his heart, you just cut open his chest. Okay, well, there's cutting and after that, you place a stone over his heart or in the cavity where his heart was, and you sew him up again. The stone has to be the same as the place you want to protect. So, cut from the ground or the same sort of stone the walls are made of, I think.

"Okay, so you have this poor drugged bugger with a stone stuck in his chest, either dead or soon about to be, and you bury him under the threshold. If you have a whole army of them, you're only supposed to put the strongest one, the leader, under the threshold, and the rest beneath the walls of the place you want to protect. And that's how you make a foundation sacrifice."

"That's it?" Catena blurted out.

Callie laughed. "Well, if you're into backyard surgery and burying people alive, yeah. Oh, wait, there's more…there's a whole second set of instructions on how to summon them when you need them. You're supposed to lift the cover stone – the threshold, or whatever they're buried under. Then you summon them to protect you." She peered at the screen, scrolling through the text. "Actually, that's all there is. The next page is all about summoning a demon protector, which looks like it uses the leftovers from the first ritual, because you need a fresh heart. Oh, ewww…." Callie shuddered.

"But isn't there anything about how you…un-summon them?"

Callie shrugged. "Nope. I guess once you've done all that work, you wouldn't want to. And if you did, you'd probably just dig up the body and burn it. Well, unless you've woken the warrior up. Then I guess you're stuck with him."

"Did you find anything about gargoyles?" Catena asked in desperation. If she couldn't free Tor…

"In this book? Nah, they weren't big on

churches, these witches. Oh, I did run across a story about a gargoyle who seduced a nun, or she seduced him, and they ran away together. Something about her love freeing him from his vigil, melting his heart of stone, so he could climb down from the roof and…well, do what gargoyles and nuns do when they've been lonely for a long time. Maybe that's why the witches used enemies in their protector summoning spells, because it's pretty hard to melt the heart of someone who wants to kill you."

That was worse than Maria's story. "So, basically, the only way to free a protector from servitude is to melt his heart of stone? Take a blowtorch to him or something?" No way was she doing that to Tor. No way in hell. He might say he was made of living stone, but she had no intention of testing where the living part ended and the stone started.

"Well, from the sound of the story, it was more of a metaphorical melting. It was a romance, after all. I imagine they probably had a few drinks, maybe shared a meal together, watched a minstrel show, he caught a glimpse of her with her hair uncovered through her chamber window and…well, gargoyles are naturally naked anyway, aren't they? Maybe he watched her from his rooftop for ages until finally he snapped. He hopped into bed with her and bam! She sucked him in with her magic pussy and freed him from durance vile!" Callie shrugged. "He doesn't sound so different to some of the guys I've dated. They start out all grumpy, but get a bit of food and alcohol into them, maybe even a suggestion of sex, and the sunshine comes out. Well, sometimes more arsehole comes out instead, and then there's no second date, but who wanted one, anyway? Online dating sites are a waste of time." Callie stared moodily at the screen. "Maybe I should try summoning a demon protector. I'm sure there's some fresh hearts in the medical school labs. It's not like I'd actually need to kill someone…"

But Catena wasn't listening. Instead, she was

forming a plan. Tonight, she'd try Callie's date method, knowing it probably wouldn't work, but until then, she'd try to frame her research as a possible PhD project and send it to Bishop. Because if it took her three years and a thesis to find a way to free Tor, she owed it to him to try. And if she earned her doctorate along the way…well, that wasn't a bad thing. And if three years wasn't enough…there were always postdocs to think of. Better get started, then.

She mumbled her thanks to Callie, and left.

FIFTY-ONE

Catena surveyed the bench. She'd probably gone overboard, but she figured it would be worth it. Jars of Persian sweets lined up, promising rose and jasmine and cardamom scented treats. Two bottles of red wine sat beside them, better stuff than she usually bought. The sparkling wine was in the fridge, ready to pop on command.

The self-saucing chocolate pudding was still

in its packaging, next to the pack of slivered hazelnuts she planned to add to it. Preparation only took a few minutes, so she left it where it was. Just as long as she remembered to take the vanilla bean ice cream out of the freezer before it got too hard to scoop.

Dinner had been the challenge. Seeing as Tor wouldn't actually eat it, she wanted something wildly aromatic, so he'd enjoy the scents, but she still had to actually cook and eat it, so it couldn't be anything too exotic.

She'd finally settled on a pizza bianca with sea salt and rosemary to start, followed by hoisin chicken with vegetables and basmati rice.

Yet as she tipped the chunks of chicken into the wok pan, then swirled it through the mix of sauces and garlic, she wondered if she should have made spaghetti bolognese instead. She could pretty much make that in her sleep, after all, but…tonight was special, or at least she wanted it to be. Tonight called for cuisine that required a little more effort.

Besides, who ever heard of breaking a spell with spaghetti bog? No. Just no.

Tor stepped into the kitchen, inhaling deeply. "What is that? The foods of this time are nothing like what I remember."

"I only wish you could taste them, too. One day, when we break this curse, I'm going to cook for you, to make up for all the meals we've shared where you couldn't." Catena took the tray of pizza bianca and slid it into the oven. "Pizza bianca. Hoisin chicken with vegetables. Rice. And dessert," she said, pointing at each in turn.

"I understood about half of that."

"It's all right. You'll remember the smells, I'm sure. Maybe you should start making a list, of what you'd like me to cook for you first."

Tor cocked his head. "You're optimistic. Did you discover something new in your research today?"

"It was my friend Callie, not me, but…maybe. I don't know if it'll work, but I figured we could try. After dinner."

"As you command, Miss Kelly." Tor ensconced himself on a bar stool.

"Ooh, you can pour the wine." She set the bottle of sparkling before him, along with two glasses.

When she returned to the bench, after vigorously stirring the chicken, she found Tor with his nose in a half-filled champagne flute.

"The bubbles tickle," he informed her. "And they smell of yeast and a little lemon, I think. Am I permitted to add drinks to this list?"

Catena smiled. "Of course. Whatever you want. This wine was one of Maria's favourites. We drank a bottle together after my graduation, and she told me the most outrageous stories about a dig at a medieval castle in France…" A blush heated her cheeks as she remembered the most outrageous of them all.

"I can't imagine the godmother you revere so greatly could have done anything that could make you blush," Tor said.

Catena almost choked. "You didn't know

her. The local men on that dig were fascinated by the Australian girl, and she had her pick of them. One night, she'd actually made assignations with two of them at the top of the tower. Now, she said she'd given them both different times, but maybe some things got lost in translation, because they all arrived at the same time."

"And the two men fought a duel for the right to her favours?" Tor guessed.

Catena snorted. "Well, I guess they sort of did cross swords, but not in the way you mean. All three of them got naked, and spent the whole night together at the top of the tower. She never would tell me the logistics of it, but she did say it was one of the most memorable nights of her life."

Tor frowned. "I fear I do not understand."

Catena patted his hand. "That's all right. I didn't really understand at the time, either, but I think I might be beginning to. One of her greatest regrets was of opportunities not taken, and she didn't want me to make the same mistake." Seduce the gargoyle. She would, if she could. Wine him, dine him, and…

Catena seized her flute and drank down the contents. Dry and yeasty, just like she remembered it. "Can you pour me another glass?"

She added the vegetables to the pan just before the oven timer chimed, and she served up the pizza bianca, setting the triangular slices on her plate and Tor's.

"This smells divine. What is it?" he asked, leaning over so far that his nose almost touched the pizza.

"It's called pizza bianca. A sort of flat bread, topped with olive oil, salt, rosemary and a little thyme. Sometimes I put other herbs on it, or garlic butter, but then it's more like garlic bread, and there's enough garlic in with the chicken."

Catena ate a couple of pieces, in between cooking and serving up the next course, as well as mixing up the pudding to pop it into the oven.

"And what is this?"

She pointed. "Well, that's rice. The rest is chicken and vegetables fried in a sweet, fermented soy sauce. You're supposed to be able to eat it with chopsticks, and of course Maria could, but I never really got the hang of them, so I tend to use a fork."

"It does indeed smell sweet, but salty and savoury, too. Most unusual. I would very much like to taste this."

All the more reason to proceed with her plan. Catena swallowed.

"Well, the offer stands. You make the list, and I'll either cook or take you to a restaurant that does a better job than I can."

When the pudding came out, Tor spent almost a full ten minutes with his face over the bowl, sniffing so hard she worried he'd inhale the sauce.

"You like that, do you?" she asked, smothering a smile.

"Do you know, I do not think I have tasted chocolate more than half a dozen times in my life? It was something rich London ladies liked to drink, or so it was said, but we could not afford such things. If it is not too much trouble, I wish to place this pudding on my list."

"No trouble at all."

She was partial to chocolate pudding, too.

Finally, she could delay no longer. She put all the dishes in the dishwasher, then poured two glasses of red wine.

"All right, Tor. It's time to try something. I have no idea if this will work, seeing as it came out of some wicked witch's spell book, but I figure anything's worth a try."

"I am yours to command, Miss Kelly."

That's what she was most afraid of. "I want you to kiss me, Tor. Like you did on the roof, when we went for our first flight together."

Tor drew back. "Are you certain, Miss Kelly?"

Fuck yes. She'd wanted him to kiss her again from the moment their lips had parted. "As certain as I am that the sun will rise tomorrow.

Kiss me, please."

He could have just leaned across the bench and pecked her on the lips. He could have, but that wasn't Tor's style.

He dismounted from his bar stool, taking deliberate steps around the bench until he stood before her.

"Take a deep breath, Miss Kelly, for once we have begun, I fear I will not be willing to let you up for air," he said.

She wanted to laugh, but she remembered how breathless their first kiss had made her, and this time he was not so tentative. So she sucked in a loud breath, then blew it out in a gust that would have extinguished a cake full of birthday candles, and granted her one wish…

This.

His lips were hard and demanding, yet still warm and yielding. For a man who did not need to breathe, he sure liked to steal her breath.

Yet she could have kissed him forever.

But she knew she had no right to keep him captive as her gargoyle protector.

Tor sensed the change in her and, contrary to his threat, let her go. "You are disappointed, Miss Kelly."

"Not about the kiss, Tor, I promise. You kiss like you should be giving lessons. Any time you want to kiss me again like that, feel free." But he wasn't free, was he? She sighed.

Tor's eyes were far too knowing. "You hoped a kiss might break the spell. I fear you have been reading too many fairy tales, Miss Kelly."

She wished he wasn't right. "Well, it was worth a try."

"Indeed it was."

Frustrated, she reached for her wine glass and gulped some down. It was a good red, too good to be thrown back like shots of cheap tequila. She took another sip.

Something that melted his heart, turning an enemy into an ally. Everyone had a price…

Catena set her glass down. Maybe Tor

would have the answer. He knew more about gargoyles than anyone else, after all. "What would it take for you to walk away from being my protector, Tor? There must be something you want, that you wish for. More than duty or anything else. What would you wish for, if you could have anything?"

Anguish darkened his eyes. "Miss Kelly, I wouldn't – "

Everyone had a price. Even Tor. He was a man, after all, even if he wasn't entirely human. "Is it killing the man who did this to you? Because if it is, I'll help you." Help him dispose of the body afterwards, too, because they'd need to, but wasn't that what friends were for? If he even considered her a friend, seeing as she'd been responsible for keeping him enslaved, by not finding a way to break the spell sooner.

"No, dear God, no! Even if that would break the spell, which I doubt, for it is likely the man has died long ago of old age, and I am still here." Tor shook his head. "I am no murderer, Miss Kelly."

Of course not. People had been hanged for murder in those days, not transported to the colonies. He'd likely only stolen a handkerchief or a loaf of bread before becoming a convict.

"Then tell me what you wish for."

"I cannot."

She threw her hands into the air. "Tor, it could be the thing that sets you free. What is so bad that you can't tell me?"

"It is too shameful."

"I once tried to stuff my brother into the letter box when he was a baby, so the postman would take him away and I could be my parents' only child again. He screamed and flailed about so much he actually gave me a black eye." She wondered if Archie remembered that. Her parents definitely did.

"Miss Kelly, that is…amusing, but nothing to be ashamed of. I'm sure all children wish to be rid of their brothers at some point. Evidently you did not succeed, unless you were not referring to the brother I met the other night..."

"No, it was Archie. Infant mortality isn't as bad as it was in your time. But we're not talking about me. We're talking about you. Your wish. The one you're too embarrassed to tell me."

"Please, Miss Kelly. I am sure anything you wished for would not be shameful. Would you tell me your greatest, most heartfelt wish?" His eyes implored, and she couldn't resist.

She only had to reflect for a moment before she had her answer. "I'd wish for one more night with Maria, here, with us, her mind as sharp as it used to be. I'd wish she could have shared this meal with us, and the wine, and then we would have taken dessert into the lounge room to watch *Stargate*. The ice cream episode, because that one was always her favourite."

Tor smiled faintly. "I, too, would have liked that."

"But it's not your greatest wish," she pressed. "The one wish that would make you leave me…"

He glared at her with such animosity she actually took a step back. "You would dismiss me for merely saying the words."

Laughter bubbled up in her chest. "Is that the answer? Like a genie, all I have to do is wish you free?"

"If you dismiss me, then I return to the darkness from whence I came to await a new call to arms. I would not be free. I would merely be gone from your sight, should you wish it." He sighed. "And you will."

"Try me, Tor. I've already promised I will find a way to set you free. Will it help if I make another promise — that whatever you tell me, however shameful your wish might be, I promise not to send you back into the dark?" Though she had to wonder where this darkness could be. He'd already said there weren't any bodies in the walls. Was he talking other dimensions, or what? If there was a gateway to hell or some dungeon dimension in her house, she definitely needed to know about it. And find a way to close it.

"You are too kind for your own good, Miss Kelly. No, such things are not fit for a lady's ears. I dare not tell you."

"I'm not a fucking lady, Tor! You've met my family. No lords or ladies among them. Just working class people, the same as you. Except they don't build mansions that will stand for centuries. Now, I've spent the morning discussing some pretty gory rituals, in the hope of finding a way to set you free. So if it's worse than cutting out hearts, summoning demons and burying people alive…just tell me, Tor."

He stood up straight, but he kept his eyes closed, as if he could not bear to look at her. "My dearest wish is to spend a night in your bed." He hung his head.

So Callie and Maria had been right. Seduce the gargoyle indeed. "That's…not so bad," she said.

Then he stared at her, his eyes wide with horror. "Do you not understand? I wish to spend the night in your bed, with you in it, doing the most debauched..." He shook his head. "It is the one thing I could do, that I long for, which would make me a complete failure as your protector. For what sort of protector would I be if I could not protect your virtue from my own dark desires? Forgive me, Miss Kelly, I would never betray you so. It is too high a price for freedom, for it would cost me not only my own honour, but your own as well."

If he hadn't been so heartbroken, this might have been funny. As it was...

She pressed her palm to his chest, over where his heart would be. "Tor, let's get one thing straight. There is nothing wrong with two – or more – consenting adults giving in to their desires. Dark or otherwise. If I've learned anything from history, it's that they always have, and they probably always will. So, if I admit I've had a few fantasies about you in my bed, too, would you be a bit more specific about what you mean when you talk about dark desires?"

She had no idea whether this would work to free him or not, but getting naked with Tor for a night…well, it was hardly a hardship.

FIFTY-TWO

She wasn't shocked. He'd told her his darkest secret and she'd asked to know more. Tor wasn't sure what to make of it.

"You're…you're naked," he whispered. "And you come and sit in my lap…"

Even with his eyes closed, he could still feel her hand on his chest. He could even feel his heart, thumping away beneath it, thrilled at her touch.

"Tor, I'll do it. I'll grant your wish, and gladly, but I have one request."

He hardly dared believe he'd heard her right. "Anything."

"If this works, or even if it doesn't, you won't walk away without at least saying goodbye, okay? Even if it's just one pre-dawn kiss, you won't just leave."

"As you wish, Miss Kelly." She would likely change her mind, but he would respect her wishes, no matter what they were.

"Yeah, and about wishes…this is your wish. I'm…look, this isn't my first time, just so you know, but I'm not really an expert at all this. I think this will work best if we go with what you want. So…you give the orders, at least for the first time."

She wanted him to give orders? How strange. He supposed he could do that.

"Take your clothes off, Miss Kelly," he began.

She gave a nod, then untied her apron and tossed it onto the bench. She toed off her shoes, kicking them into a corner, before she lifted the hem of her dress. Up and up and up, until she dragged the dress over her head and dropped it on the floor. She bit her lip, looking nervous standing there in little more than a corset and stockings. Good God. Did women not wear drawers in this time? Oh, but there was a tiny scrap of lace at the juncture of her thighs, in the same deep blue as the trim on her corset.

He couldn't help but stare. He wanted to drink her in, to taste…

His mouth was dry. He wanted to reach for a glass of wine and pour it down his throat. Not that it would help. He wanted to bite through that scrap of lace and taste her. His pants were growing uncomfortably tight. If he didn't remove them soon, the pain would become unbearable.

She gestured at her corset. It sat against her bare skin, with no underthings at all. Scandalous. And yet…perfect.

"I bought this for a steampunk festival a few

years back. I haven't worn it since. I'm surprised it still fits..."

"Take it off." His own words surprised him. They sounded so raw.

"I...okay." A faint smile touched her lips, one filled with mischief. "Yes, Mr Stone." She began to undo the row of buttons fastening the front. Each one gave a little pop as she released it, and her creamy flesh began to spill out the top. Bit by glorious bit, until her breasts were completely exposed, the nipples like two pink jewels. He'd never seen anything so perfect.

The pants had to go, or he was going to burst the stitching. He ripped the lacing in his eagerness, and the pants dropped to the floor. He kicked them away, then dragged a dining chair away from the table so that he might sit on it while he watched her.

With one final pop, the corset released her. Never had he imagined such beauty, not even in his dreams.

"You are the most beautiful woman I have

ever seen, Miss Kelly."

She grinned. "You're pretty sexy yourself." She eyed his groin with approval.

He did not want her eyes on him. He wanted to feel her flesh against his.

"Come here and sit on my lap," he said, patting his thigh. He half expected her to panic or refuse, or at least hesitate.

But Miss Kelly was a marvel. She picked her way across the floor, through the maze of discarded clothing, until she stood before him. Then she set her hands on his shoulders, curled one leg around his hip, then the other, as she settled in his lap.

Rough lace scratched against his tender flesh. She hadn't taken off her tiny drawers. He stuck two fingers inside the ribbon of fabric at her hip, and ripped. Then he did the same with the other side, before throwing the ripped rags to the floor.

"Pity. I liked those," she said.

"I asked you to take your clothes off."

"Well, you could have warned me you'd rip

them off if I didn't."

He didn't know what to say to that. He hadn't known how much it would anger him, having that miserable scrap of lace standing between them.

"I'll just remember for next time," she said, her voice a little breathy as she rubbed against him. "What…what next?"

Tor couldn't seem to find any words for her. Just the feel of her skin against his, rubbing along his length as she shifted in his lap. He wrapped his wings around her, holding tight, then urging her forward before pulling her back, over and over until the mesmerising rhythm of her movements was all he could think about. Her slick heat, so tantalisingly close. If he just tilted his hips a little and thrust…

Catena arched her back and cried out. It was the most joyful sound he'd ever heard – and he'd done that, he'd driven her to the heights of ecstasy. Her cry had barely died away before he was determined to hear it again. His own pleasure could wait, especially while he was the master of hers.

Her breasts bounced before his face, and he surrendered to temptation, taking one of those jewel-like nipples between his teeth as he cupped those gorgeous globes in both hands. Silken soft, he couldn't seem to stop stroking them.

She cried out a second time, her thighs tightening around him. She was panting now, her eyes half lidded as she stared at him in wonder.

He tore his lips from her breast and kissed her instead. She kissed him back with the sort of desperation that matched his own. If they were to share but this one night together, then there would be no holding back.

He felt her stiffen, her back arching again, but he did not release her lips, swallowing her cries as another orgasm shook her body.

She was the most beautiful, the most perfect, the sweetest… He opened his mouth to tell her.

"Tor, please," she gasped out. "Please, I need to feel you inside me. Now, Tor, before you give me another…argh…another…"

His wings lifted her as he shifted, then lowered her to give her what she wanted. Molten silk sliding around him, encasing him, as she pressed down, down, until he was sheathed to the hilt in the sweetest, most perfect woman who had ever lived.

FIFTY-THREE

Catena teetered on the brink of her fourth orgasm, sucking in a breath to scream because she knew this one would be bigger than the rest, she could feel it, just as she could feel his hard length beneath her as she rubbed against him, teasing her, but not giving her what she wanted, not yet.

Then he lifted her, the slightest chill of air between them before he impaled her, the slowest and most exquisite torture imaginable. Inch by glorious inch, he filled her, hotter and harder than any human flesh, until she felt she might split in two. Until…she was sitting in his lap again, his massive cock (for this was no mere dick or penis, no, the monster wedged tightly inside her was a fully-fledged cock) stretching her to her very limits.

She trembled, hardly daring to move, because if she did, she'd combust into a million stars, and she didn't want to miss even a moment of the best sex of her life.

Tor smiled knowingly, as if he could read her thoughts. Perhaps he could, for his wings lifted her again, the length of him stroking all of her most intimate walls, before he slammed her back down again. Once. Twice. Three t…

The unearthly scream that rent the air could not have come from a human throat, let alone hers, but it must have. She was clenched down so hard on him, she'd have snapped a normal man's dick off.

Yet Tor just sat there, chuckling, the rumble

of his laughter making her insides quake in the most delightful way. "I had thought to take you to bed before you'd scream so," he said, shaking his head.

Bed! Yes. They could do so much more there. But her legs were boneless after that earth-shattering orgasm. "I don't think I can walk yet," she admitted, feeling her cheeks heat.

With another roar of laughter, he rose to his feet, lifting her effortlessly along with him. She wrapped her legs tightly around his hips as she felt him start to slip out, just as he adjusted his grip on her, driving him in deeper, making her gasp and see stars.

By the time her vision cleared, he was lowering her onto the bed, his wings cradling her body as he knelt between her spread thighs. Then he lifted her legs, so her knees bent over his shoulders.

"You've offered me many treats tonight that I could smell and not taste, but there is one cup I cannot refuse. I will not let this night end before I have tasted you, and drunk deep."

And then there were no words, for his tongue was too busy, and his fingers, and his lips...waves of pleasure overcame her, as relentless as the ocean itself, until she could stand no more, and she begged for his cock again.

Grinning, Tor wiped his mouth with the back of his hand. His wings lowered her, so her back touched the bed again, but he didn't shift her legs off his shoulders. She felt his hot, hard head touch her clit, but go no further.

"Those are the sweetest, saltiest words I ever heard fall from a lady's lips, Miss Kelly, and I believe I would like to hear you say them again."

She didn't know what she'd said. Just that she needed him, now. "I want...I need...to feel your cock inside me again. I want you to fuck me until I forget my own name and all I can scream is yours. Please, Tor, I need to feel you inside me now."

With one swift thrust, he granted her wish,

but then he slowed. He pumped into her, slow and dark and deep, a pace as relentless as the beat of her own heart. As she looked into his eyes, fixed on her, though there was only one heart between them, they shared it equally, two bodies moving as one.

Until he leaned in to whisper, "I love you."

Tears sprang to her eyes as she fought to find the breath to say the same words back to him. She knew it down to her bones, but she couldn't...seem to...

Oh God, she was close to the cliff again. So close...

"Come for me, Miss Kelly," Tor growled.

"Come with me, Mr Stone," she puffed back, clenching down hard as her whole body seemed to dissolve.

She smiled as she heard him roar his release.

Whatever else their future held – freedom for him, she hoped – at least she would have no regrets about this night.

FIFTY-FOUR

The clink of chains woke Tor from his doze. He must have moved in his sleep. The guards did not even remove the chains to allow him to sleep. If they did not remove them soon, he would die in chains, locked within the walls he had built, long before their shoddy workmanship fell apart.

He had dreamed this moment many times in the darkness, despair dragging him down deeper until he could not escape, but tonight, it was different.

"Get up," Dunstan whispered.

Arms at his shoulders dragged him from his hammock, forcing him to his feet.

"Wrap this around them so they don't make that infernal noise."

It was a blanket they'd wrapped around his chains, he remembered now, to muffle the sounds they made with every step he took. Then they marched him out of the barracks, to the smithy at the back of the prison.

Never had the ring of a hammer on stone sounded sweeter than when Ben's blow shattered his chains. His little brother, his apprentice, setting him free.

"We have made a deal with the butcher. He will help all three of us escape, but we must go tonight," Ben said, poking a bit of wire into Tor's manacles. He wiggled it a bit, and they popped open. Within minutes, Tor was free.

It was a terrible thing indeed, to take pride in his brother's skill at picking locks, for he never would have learned it had they not been arrested and transported here. Yet they were here, and if they could escape and be free, perhaps they could make a life here, just as they'd planned.

"Thank you," Tor said, rubbing his wrists. The manacles were gone, but he still felt their weight. Maybe he always would.

"We could hardly escape without you. All three of us go free, or none at all," Dunstan declared.

Tor's heart swelled with love, at the loyalty of his brothers. Yes. They would all be free. Miss Kelly would help them…

Miss Kelly. He could not leave Miss Kelly. He'd promised.

They would understand. His brothers had known what it was to love a woman. Dunstan with his misplaced passion for the innkeeper's daughter, though she played him false, and Ben with his misguided infatuation for that wretched woman who had gotten them into this mess in the first place.

They would understand that he could not leave the woman he loved.

Tor turned again, letting out a sigh of contentment as the chains no longer clinked, for they were broken on the smith's anvil, discarded on the ground. And Catena was here in his arms, her warm body just a breath away. Better than he deserved. Almost like a dream…

Tor drifted off again, his dreams far fairer than they had any right to be.

FIFTY-FIVE

Catena woke in the predawn light, with the warm weight of Tor still asleep in the bed beside her. Huh, so gargoyles did sleep after all. Or maybe just after a marathon sex session. She slid out of bed, careful not to wake him, and walked stiffly to the study.

She'd made up her mind. She would apply to do her PhD project on things hidden in houses, and other buildings here in Western

Australia. And when, not if, she found what she needed to free Tor, she'd share it with him so he could live the life he deserved.

After last night, she hoped he'd be willing to share at least some of that life with her, but she didn't want to be too greedy. He deserved to choose his own path, after sleeping through so many years.

She jotted down a summary of the project in an email to Bishop, then sent the whole proposal off to him. If she didn't get a scholarship, she might still be able to scrape by on her librarian's salary, plus the rent from the shops downstairs, now she owned the building and all. Whatever. She'd work things out. She owed it to Tor.

The sun had risen while she'd been working, and her stomach was bellyaching about wanting breakfast, or at least coffee. She peeked into the bedroom on her way past, to find the bed empty.

He was gone. No kiss, no goodbye, nothing. Swallowing back tears that threatened to overwhelm her, she dragged her heavy heart to the kitchen. She'd have Irish coffee with her breakfast this morning, and bugger anybody who dared to complain about it. It wasn't like there was anyone here who could complain.

She stepped through the kitchen doorway, and for a moment, it felt like her heart stopped.

Tor stood in front of the fridge, holding the baking dish in one hand. With his other hand, he scooped up an enormous spoonful of chocolate pudding and stuck it in his mouth. Then he licked the spoon clean. Every swipe of his tongue sent echoes through her lady bits, memories of what he'd done to her with that tongue last night.

Her mouth dropped open.

"That's...not a breakfast food," was all she managed to say. Then again, if she'd seen it first, she probably would have eaten it herself this morning. Chocolate pudding beat Irish coffee, hands down.

"Now, the ladies in London had chocolate

every morning for breakfast, my mother used to tell me, though how she knew is a mystery. Maybe she made it up to amuse my little brother, who was always fascinated by stories of what the quality got up to. Mum was a gentleman's granddaughter, but her cousins were the ones with all the money, not her side of the family, so none of them made a fuss when she married Dad, who was just a farmer. Never thought I'd be eating breakfast like a London lady here in the colonies, though." The spoon tinkled into the empty baking dish before he set it in the sink. "You look like you could use some coffee, or maybe some chocolate. If you have any more, that is." A beam of sunlight shot through the kitchen window and hit him squarely in the face. Tor raised an arm to shield his eyes. "Gah, but that's bright. I'd forgotten how brutal the Australian sun can be."

She couldn't seem to close her mouth. It just...wouldn't...

"Forgive me for my rudeness, Miss Kelly. I

have not yet wished you good morning, or enquired after your health. Where are my manners?" He cleared his throat. "Good day, Miss Kelly. I trust you slept well?"

She tried to speak, but all she could do was splutter.

His eyes turned grave. "I see how it is, and I am not surprised, though I won't deny I wish things might have been otherwise. I thank you for your kind hospitality, Miss Kelly, and I wish you all the best for your future health and happiness." He bowed, and headed for the door.

Was he quoting Jane Austen at her? He was hardly a Darcy.

"Don't go! Please!" she blurted out.

He managed a smile, but it did not reach the sadness in his eyes. "I know when I have outstayed my welcome, Miss Kelly, and it is clear that you regret the unfortunate events of last night. I can offer no excuse for my behaviour, for it was as if I was under a spell, but I can tender my sincerest apologies for any unpleasantness I may have caused you…"

"Six orgasms were not unpleasant!" She felt her cheeks grow hot. Of all the things to say…

Another bow. "I am delighted to hear it, Miss Kelly." He didn't sound it, though. And he was still edging toward the door. Leaving her.

"Tor, please, at least let me make you a coffee. Or tea. I think I still have some hot chocolate, if you haven't had enough already…" Now she was babbling. She stamped her foot. "Damn it, I don't want you to go. I don't regret what we did last night, though I would like some more sleep, and…what happened to your wings?"

Only now did she realise they were missing.

"Stolen from me as I slept, or some such thing," he said cheerfully. "I woke up without them, but with the most enormous appetite, so I hied myself to your kitchen and…availed myself of your hospitality."

"And the sun…doesn't hurt you any more…" she said slowly.

"I would not say that. It's just as blinding as I remember. Why, with all the limestone dust in the streets, getting into our eyes, tearing up in the sun, it's a miracle more of us did not go blind. My youngest brother, Ben, would use up half his water ration, washing the grit from his eyes, he was that worried about it. He had the makings of a great artist, and he meant to become one…"

Realisation dawned. "You're free. You even have your memories back. Whatever we did last night broke the curse. You're free!" She threw her arms around him, and was surprised that he didn't feel any different. Well, except for the wings, he was just as warm and hard as ever. "What do you want to do first?"

He grinned impishly. "Well, I don't rightly know. Last night, you had me making a list…"

Catena blinked. "Oh, we still have leftovers from dinner, if you like."

That grin turned devilish. "After you fell asleep, I rearranged the list in my head, so to speak. I decided that the one thing I wanted to taste first was the chocolate sauce from that pudding. I wanted to lick it off your bare breasts."

She swallowed. He was looking at her like he had last night. If he ordered her to undress again…there were definitely going to be more clothes on the floor. "I think I have a bottle of chocolate sauce in the pantry…" Shaky legs carried her over to the door, and she had to hold onto it to stay upright as she scanned the shelves, unseeing, until her eyes focussed on two bottles, tucked behind a big packet of sprinkles. Before she could second guess herself, she grabbed all three.

She held out a bottle to Tor. "This one's for you."

He looked askance at the other one.

She wet her lips. "I have some wishes that involve licking, too." She let her gaze drift down his chest, his abs, and the pants she really didn't want him to be wearing right now.

FIFTY-SIX

Several hours later, after taking a steamy shower and cleaning up the sticky mess of sprinkles all over the dining room table, Catena noticed a new email from Bishop in her inbox. It consisted of five words: SEE ME IN MY OFFICE.

She sighed. He was going to shout at her again, she knew it.

Now she needed a protector at her side, the

position was vacant.

"Ha, I know that look! It's the peculiar expression you get when someone is about to start shouting, as though you want to run and hide." Tor grinned at her. "I swear I have no reason to shout at you, and though I am not officially your protector any more, I do feel a peculiar responsibility to uphold your honour, even if my own actions thus far have been less than honourable..." He coughed, then cleared his throat. "Allow me to make amends, Miss Kelly. After robbing you of your virtue, I feel it only fitting that I should ask for your hand in marriage, so that you do not suffer any ill consequences from the spell that defied both your and my good judgement last night. So, Miss Kelly, as I believe you are above the age of consent, will you..."

"No." She almost laughed at his shocked expression. "Times have changed, Tor, as I keep telling you. I haven't been a virgin for quite a number of years now, so I'm pretty sure there was no virtue for you to steal. If by ill consequences you mean an unplanned pregnancy, that's not going to happen, either, because this is the age of contraception, which means I have a little injection once every few months, and don't need to worry about that. Even if I did, being a single mother is perfectly acceptable in this day and age, and under no circumstances do I need a husband to take care of me." She softened. "But, in a few years, if you stick around and get to know me better, and maybe you decide you want to ask me again, I would not be averse to the idea of marriage."

His frown didn't lighten. "But we have shared a bed, Miss Kelly, in the most vigorous fashion. I hope I am not too forward in suggesting that the desire to do so again might grow too strong to resist. But if we are married…"

There was still so much she'd have to explain about her time, and how different it was to the world Tor had known. "Tor, I love you. The sex is amazing, and I want to have a lot more of it with you. Tonight, if possible, and tomorrow, too. I think you're a wonderful man and I want you to stay with me, if that's what you want. I really can make up one of the guest rooms, if that would make you feel more comfortable. But I am not going to marry a man I've only known for two weeks. Two years, maybe."

"So, am I to understand that in this time, pouring chocolate and sprinkles into and licking them out of unmentionable places is acceptable, but a short courtship is not?"

His abs were not an unmentionable place. Still, she said, "Yes."

He nodded gravely, his mind evidently turning it all over before he spoke. Finally, he said, "Very well. And what of other things? Will you permit me to protect you during the two years we must spend courting, before I am allowed to ask for your hand?"

No way was she going to be able to keep refusing him for two years. Best that she didn't tell him that, though.

"I don't really need much protecting, but if you were to come with me to a meeting with my research supervisor at the university and maybe loom protectively, I would be grateful," she admitted.

His eyes narrowed. "Chocolate and sprinkles grateful?"

She laughed. "I'll have to go to the supermarket for more sauce and sprinkles, but, yes, I'll definitely give you another blow job."

"Only if you allow me to reciprocate."

"Of course."

If they kept this up, the clothes were going to come off again, she was going to dig out that last bottle of butterscotch sauce, and they'd have to clean the kitchen again.

"Look, let's go meet with him now and get this over with. Then we can go out for dinner, I can introduce you to tacos and the sheer decadence that is queso, at the Mexican Kitchen up on the Terrace, and we can swing by the supermarket before we come home."

Tor inclined his head, then held out his arm,

like something out of an Austen movie. "Miss Kelly?"

She laughed, grabbed her bag, and headed out onto High Street with him.

FIFTY-SEVEN

The moment she entered Bishop's office, he beckoned her to his desk. "Sit," he said.

She did. Tor took the seat beside her.

"Now tell me where and how you came up with this project. And keep your voice down. My soon to be ex-wife finally agreed to a divorce settlement last night, and I was up all night celebrating. Must have had a bad batch, what with the headache I have this morning."

She wasn't surprised he had a hangover – Bishop's capacity for drink at the department Christmas parties had long since passed into legend. For a celebration this momentous…he'd have drunk enough to drown an army.

Catena explained about the shoes, and how it had led her to identify the West Australian sized gap in the current research on the subject. She didn't mention the part about gargoyles. Luckily, neither did Tor.

"So, will you sign off on it?" she asked anxiously.

"It's a low budget project with high media value, plus think of all the papers you could write, with so many sites! You know if you write enough papers, you can just staple them all together and submit that instead of your thesis? I've already put out a call to all my colleagues for anything in their investigations that might qualify as hidden objects, and you'll want to contact the National Trust. So many heritage conservation projects going on at the moment with the government funding to help prop up the construction industry. I've spoken to the board, and while it's not official yet, they've all given their approval. In fact, there's a couple of top up scholarships you might want to put in for, on top of the one you originally applied for, because it's a good idea to get as much funding as possible while your project is the flavour of the month..." He went on for a bit longer, but Catena didn't need to hear the rest. He'd put it all in an email later, if he hadn't drafted it already.

Finally, he stood up to shake her hand. "I look forward to working with you on this project, Miss Kelly." He was smiling at her, but she knew what he really saw were all the potential citations, because his name would be on those papers, too.

She didn't mind. She thanked him, and followed Tor out the door to the taco place.

FIFTY-EIGHT

After tacos, they stopped for ice cream on the way home. Poor Tor wanted to try every flavour, but settled for the rum and raisin, swearing he'd be back to try the rest. Catena didn't doubt it.

"Are you sure you don't mind sharing your lovely home with an ex-convict?" Tor asked. He'd finally admitted to it over dinner, though she'd pretty much come to that conclusion anyway, so it had hardly come as a surprise.

"You've been living in my house for longer than I've been alive, and you've been the most well-behaved housemate I've ever had for the last two weeks. As long as you're not planning to do anything illegal, I'm sure we'll be fine," she said.

"That thing with the sprinkles…"

"Not illegal, as long as we don't do it in public."

"I like this time!"

With Tor by her side, ice cream in her hand, and a PhD project and scholarship on the horizon, Catena had to admit she was quite fond of it, too.

"So, what do you plan to do, now that you're free of your chains, Tor?" she asked, then added, "After tonight, of course."

"Ah." He took a big bite from his ice cream, without even wincing at the cold against his teeth. "My memories have started to come back, and I believe I may have mentioned to you that I have, or had, two brothers, who were transported with me to the Swan River Colony. The night I escaped, they came with me, and they also met with the butcher named Pearse, who hid us in the cellar of his home. My last memory is of the three of us together in the cellar, before the butcher turned me into the man you summoned to your aid that night.

"My brothers. I wish to know what became of them. Did they become gargoyles, too, bound to serve other masters? If so, then I must find a way to free them."

If they could actually pin down what they'd done that had freed Tor. They still weren't sure.

"But first, I must find them. Will you be willing to assist me? Your knowledge of this world is far superior to mine. Perhaps in the aether, you can find a picture of them."

Finding a picture on the internet, among the billions on there. That was like making a video go viral, when most of them only ever got a few views and died an ignominious death. If only that had happened to the Moth Man.

"I'll see what I can do. I'll probably be better at finding a way to free them, seeing as that's one of the things I'll be studying as part of my PhD research. I can't believe a pair of old shoes could be such good luck." Catena shook her head.

"I would very much like to see these lucky shoes," Tor said.

Catena frowned. "I thought you already had. I mean, you were there when I found the second one."

Tor shook his head slowly. "You instructed me to stay out of your neighbour's house. I never would have disobeyed such a firm order, especially not when I might alarm the poor widow."

"But there was a penis. Your penis, sticking out of the wall. I saw it for only a moment, before it vanished. Into the wall, just like you do. Or you did, anyway." She stared at him. "That wasn't your penis? I was staring at some other gargoyle's penis?" She burst out laughing. "I bet it was him dancing on the roof, too! I'm so sorry I blamed you, Tor." She eyed the frown on his face. "You have forgiven me for that, right?"

"Miss Kelly, would you show me that movie of the Moth Man dancing again, please?" he asked.

"Sure." She pulled out her phone, and found the video. He did have some moves, that other gargoyle. Now she knew Tor's body better, she could definitely see it wasn't him. The other gargoyle was more wiry, with less bulk. Maria had mentioned the gargoyle in the house, and how she regretted not seducing him, but Tor had denied ever meeting Maria or of having any memories of being awake between 1855 and the present day. But if she'd met this dancing gargoyle, maybe…

"Miss Kelly, I believe this might be my older brother, Dunstan. He was always a most determined flirt and he was as deft at dancing as I was clumsy. If he was indeed on your rooftop, then it is possible he, too, has taken up residence in your house."

Catena quickened her steps toward home. "Shit, Tor, we have to warn Anemone!"

ABOUT THE AUTHOR

Demelza Carlton has always loved the ocean, but on her first snorkelling trip she found she was afraid of fish.

She has since swum with sea lions, sharks and sea cucumbers and stood on spray drenched cliffs over a seething sea as a seven-metre cyclonic swell surged in, shattering a shipwreck below.

Demelza now lives in Perth, Western Australia, the shark attack capital of the world.

The *Ocean's Gift* series was her first foray into fiction, followed by her suspense thriller *Nightmares* trilogy. She swears the *Mel Goes to Hell* series ambushed her on a crowded train and wouldn't leave her alone.

Want to know more? You can follow Demelza on Facebook, Twitter, YouTube or her website, Demelza Carlton's Place at:

www.demelzacarlton.com

Books by Demelza Carlton

Siren of Secrets series

Ocean's Secret (#1)
Ocean's Gift (#2)
Ocean's Infiltrator (#3)

Siren of War series

Ocean's Justice (#1)
Ocean's Widow (#2)
Ocean's Bride (#3)
Ocean's Rise (#4)
Ocean's War (#5)
How To Catch Crabs

Nightmares Trilogy

Nightmares of Caitlin Lockyer (#1)
Necessary Evil of Nathan Miller (#2)
Afterlife of Alana Miller (#3)

Mel Goes to Hell series

The Devil's Work (#1)
See You in Hell (#2)
Mel Goes to Hell (#3)
To Hell and Back (#4)
The Holiday From Hell (#5)
All Hell Breaks Loose (#6)
The Devil Goes to Heaven (#7)

Romance Island Resort series

Maid for the Rock Star (#1)
The Rock Star's Email Order Bride (#2)
The Rock Star's Virginity (#3)
The Rock Star and the Billionaire (#4)
The Rock Star Wants A Wife (#5)
The Rock Star's Wedding (#6)
Maid for the South Pole (#7)

Romance a Medieval Fairytale series

Enchant: Beauty and the Beast Retold
Dance: Cinderella Retold
Fly: Goose Girl Retold
Revel: Twelve Dancing Princesses Retold
Silence: Little Mermaid Retold
Awaken: Sleeping Beauty Retold
Embellish: Brave Little Tailor Retold
Appease: Princess and the Pea Retold
Blow: Three Little Pigs Retold
Return: Hansel and Gretel Retold
Wish: Aladdin Retold
Melt: Snow Queen Retold
Spin: Rumpelstiltskin Retold
Kiss: Frog Prince Retold
Reflect: Snow White Retold
Roar: Goldilocks Retold
Cobble: Elves and the Shoemaker Retold
Float: Enchanted Horse Retold
Steal: Forty Thieves Retold
Call: Pied Piper Retold

Feather: Swan Maidens Retold
Curse: Rose Red Retold
Cross: Three Billy Goats Gruff Retold
Weave: Rapunzel Retold
Claim: Puss in Boots Retold

Colony Universe

Cowboys and Aliens
Ghost
Vulcan
Cupid
Valentine
Prometheus
Halcyon
Poseidon
Apollo

Heart of Stone series

Broken Chains
Broken Bonds
Broken Dreams

Heart of Steel series

Stone Guardian
Stone Champion
Stone Sentinel
Stone Shadow

www.ingramcontent.com/pod-product-compliance
Lightning Source LLC
Chambersburg PA
CBHW070421170726
48291CB00002B/303